BESS TRULY
AND THE
HYALINE
SHARK

BY JOE SLEDGE

North Carolina

Gravity Well Books

Publisher

For Callie

Contents

Thursday, August 16th, 1956
The Outer Banks of North Carolina

CHAPTER 1

A Quick Beach Trip

The skies cleared to a beautiful mix of blue and white as Bess Truly and her father Steve Truly piloted the Starlighter over the thick green trees of North Carolina's coastal plains. It was so different from her home of Three Winds, New Mexico. Bess was used to the flat and open land of Three Winds and the prairie stretched out as far as she could see. Visitors to her state just called the land a desert without ever seeing the life all around in the open prairie. But now, Bess and her father were enthralled with the view beneath them.

The trees grew tall and richly green. Bess knew they were Carolina Pines, giant prickly trees that grew in abundance across the state. Through the trees, they could just barely see the roads that cut through the state. More obvious were the many small streams and creeks that cut into the woods with dark water the color of tea.

Bess sat in her chair in the cockpit of the Starlighter, her father's specially built aircraft. It was unlike any airplane in the world. Shaped like a razor thin disc, many people took it for a flying saucer. Bess often bristled as she corrected anyone who called the Starlighter that. It flew by using a static charge from batteries stored in the center of the craft. A bright electric pop would go off at a regular beat, a heartbeat, Bess always imagined, which heated the air underneath the craft, which then lifted the Starlighter into the air. A thin ring around the outside of the aircraft spun at a high rate of speed to keep it stable, while sets of winglets in the middle all around the cockpit steered the Starlighter. It was fast, light, and highly maneuverable. It could fly like a helicopter or faster than most planes.

The only limitation it had was distance. The batteries could only provide enough power for about thirty minutes flight time. Steve and Bess had discovered ways to lengthen the time, by letting the Starlighter glide in the air, and some new launching pads, but they still were limited by the weight and size of the battery and the craft itself.

Still, flying at 500 miles per hour meant that they could cover a lot of distance in a short time.

It had taken a lot of work to arrange for a trip of 1800 miles from New Mexico to the east coast of the United States. Bess's family, her pilot father Steve and physicist mother Portia, who had invented the engine for the Starlighter, had arranged a collection of generators, landing and take off pads, and the trucks needed to haul all the equipment from state to state in order to take this trip. It was something that was important to Steve. They were taking the Starlighter all the way to the Outer Banks of North Carolina to be on the islands for Orville Wright's birthday, which was also National Aviation Day.

The flights had been short, but wonderful for Bess and her father. Once they crossed Oklahoma and Texas, the ground beneath them began to change. Gone was the dusty beige of the prairie and the open flatlands of the west. The colors changed to red clay soil that had been turned up by plows for farmland, and patches of twisted field trees that were left to define borders of properties as they passed over the states of Tennessee and Georgia. Skirting below the tall Appalachian Mountains that were the western part of North Carolina, Bess and Steve Truly had stopped outside of Greenville, South Carolina before flying on to Raleigh, the capital of North Carolina, to spend the night.

The next day had been a fun visit to the city for Bess. Raleigh was different from her state capital of Santa Fe. There were no chili peppers, but lots of chili flakes and pigs. North Carolina was proud of its tasty chopped up barbecue, which was tangy and tender. Bess enjoyed it, but her friend Jesse Armstrong loved it. Jesse, a year older than Bess, had worked with her father arranging the trucks that drove the generators and chargers for the Starlighter across the country. Jesse loved cars, driving, and anything mechanical, so he had jumped at the chance to help when Bess's father had asked if he wanted to join in.

"I wonder if you can freeze this stuff and take it back home," he joked as the two of them ate an early lunch. "My dad would love this. He would figure out a way to open up a 'barbecue joint' in Three Winds." Jesse's father owned several small businesses in their hometown. Three Winds was a nice town that had started as a watering hole for travelers. It now had a school and parks, along with a radio station, movie theater, and ice cream parlor that Jesse's father ran for the local kids.

Raleigh was so different. It was a planned city from about two hundred years earlier. It was built to be the capital. Bess had learned quickly that it was the home of a large university, North Carolina State, and that there were two other colleges, Duke University and the University of North Carolina Chapel Hill, were both nearby. She discovered that when she landed the evening before and a large group of students were waiting at the airport to see the Starlighter. Jesse had already talked her up to the students, while older pilots stood back, doubtful of the description of the Starlighter, but still curious. They wanted to see how the 'flying saucer' would fly, if it was really as fast as the kid on the ground crew claimed. They stood back, aloof, hiding behind sunglasses in the light of an August sunset, mumbling to one another. The college students were more animated as they bounced around, talking loudly and excitedly.

When the Starlighter had finally appeared, everyone got quiet quickly. Then they all cried out in surprise. Bess was piloting it, and she came in over the cleared airport of Raleigh-Durham as fast as she could. The Starlighter whipped through the air, its engine pulsing in the yellowing sly. A purple gleam popped under the shining silver of the Starlighter. The point in the bottom of the craft sent an electric spark out, heating up the underside of the Starlighter, which gave the aircraft its name. A thin ring spun at high speed to help cut through the air and keep the ship stable. Bess flew over the landing pad at high speed before turning the Starlighter on its edge, the little winglets shimmering in the sun as they popped and rattled to slow the craft down. She flew it onto its side, so that the edge was perpendicular to the ground. The high speed braking created circular vortices around the entire ring. Bess knew it was a spectacular sight that wowed the crowds when they landed.

On the ground, Jesse wasn't disappointed. The group of college students and adult pilots all 'Ooooh!'ed at the same time. The sound was a harmony of youthful exuberance, and deep adult voices. Everyone was impressed, and Jesse knew the pilots were a little jealous. They would feel even more jealous when they saw a fifteen year old girl get out of the cockpit.

So Bess, Jesse, and Steve Truly all had to stay around the airport until late that night to answer all the questions and show off how the Starlighter worked. They had flown a little over 200 miles, but had left South Carolina quickly, so the Starlighter needed a full night to charge back up. The evening had gone on into night, with lots of questions from the students for Bess, while she tried to get in a few questions of her own about what college life was like in North Carolina. Jesse asked about what there was to do on the beaches. He was very excited about seeing the ocean for the first time.

The next morning had been tough on all of them. The time changed from New Mexico to North Carolina where the sun came up hours earlier. Everyone was tired and they all slept in until after 9 am. A late breakfast and some time to wander around the city was a change of pace for Bess. Jesse had already planned a visit for them to the Museum of History where they saw whale skeletons and the teeth of giant extinct sharks. Jesse was impressed. "Wow, do you think we'll see anything like that when we get to the coast?"

Bess stared at the giant jaw of a long extinct 40 foot shark, then looked up to see the skeletons of huge whales that once swam offshore in the Atlantic Ocean.

"I doubt it," she looked at the plaque near the big shark teeth. "This says the Megalodon went extinct about 4 million years ago."

Jesse almost seemed disappointed. "It says here that people occasionally find their teeth washed up on the beaches. Hey, maybe you'll find one!"

"That would be an interesting souvenir," Jesse agreed.

An hour later, Jesse was doing his best impression of a shark by eating a large plate of the local delicacy, North Carolina barbecue.

"Eastern barbecue," Jesse had corrected. "They have two kinds. This is eastern. They use vinegar and chili flakes," he said between bites.

So with a full belly, Bess and Jesse had returned to the airport to fly on their last journey to the coast of North Carolina. They were running late and now had to hurry. The flight may not take long, if they flew at high speed, but Bess wanted to enjoy the view. The only issue they had was a storm coming in from the west and south. They should be able to outrun it, but storms in the south, where it got hot and humid in the afternoons, were notorious for popping up out of clear skies. The land they would fly over might be flat, but it was a mix of thick tree forest and wide rivers than emptied into large open bays. "They call them sounds here," Steve had explained while looking over a map.

The Starlighter was taking off to a even larger crowd the next afternoon. "RDU tower, this is NX4400 Special, Starlighter, requesting takeoff clearance." Steve Truly had the wonderfully confident voice of a pilot who has done this thousands of times. Bess knew it would have been at least several hundred, including his time as a fighter pilot during World War II. "NX4400, you are clear for takeoff," came the singsong voice that all pilots recognized.

"Up and out, kiddo?" asked Steve. It was his usual comment to Bess when they flew.

"Let's touch the sky, Dad," she responded. They launched the Starlighter into the clear blue afternoon with a rapid series of pops of white light from under the ship, as the ring spun fast and smooth around the outer edge. The Starlighter shot up into the sky and flew off to the east, racing away from the dark clouds behind her.

It was with that departure and flight that the two pilots found them now humming along the inland coast of North Carolina. Bess had looked down at the trees that covered the land, only broken by an upcoming river. Steve looked at his map as they slowed the Starlighter to a near hover to take in the view.

"It's called the Alligator River," he said as he traced a blue line on the map.

"Do you think there are alligators there for real?" Bess asked. She had never seen an alligator before.

"I doubt it. I thought they just were in Florida. But there is the name right there, so maybe so."

The two were so busy looking at the view that they didn't notice the dark clouds coming up from the south, chasing up the big open river. Dark skies closed in on the land behind them. Far below, the Alligator River went from a shiny smooth blue chrome to dark, all green and brown, with little white waves topping off from the wind. Steve glanced out the back of the big open canopy of the Starlighter to see a frontal line coming toward them.

"We better get going," he said, as he reached for the collective to speed up the Starlighter. "We may be in for some weather..."

Off in the distance, a crackle of lightning bent its way between the clouds and the ground. There was no sound that penetrated the Starlighter, as the hum of its ring and the general *thump thump thump* of the engine hid any sound from outside. The lightning was too far away, anyhow, to be heard.

CrackBOOM!

The next bolt was much much closer!

CHAPTER 2

Like Lightning

There was a crackle and loud boom that shook the Starlighter from behind, just as Steve pushed the throttle forward. The cockpit filled with a white and blue light, like someone had just taken a picture outside the cockpit. Steve and Bess had the strange sensation of being thrown forward into empty space as the Starlighter pulsed its way forward, and away from the approaching storm.

Bess felt herself float just above her seat until her body caught up with the strange acceleration and the whipcrack of the lightning bolt. She glanced around the cockpit first. There were no signs that the Starlighter was in trouble on her instruments. She and her father each had the same set of dials and lights, so he could see, too, that the Starlighter was still flying. Then Bess glanced outside. She was sure she would see either a hole pierced in the hard metal of her aircraft, or at least a tree by the river smoking from the close strike. Fortunately, nothing appeared to be wrong outside, either.

Her body caught up with the seat and she felt herself sink into the familiar leather of the pilot chair. "Whoooah…" she said, softly, as the Starlighter rose up and did a little flutter, then catching itself with a big soft puff of air under its winglets. Like the clear air turbulence and downdrafts of other planes, the Starlighter felt them, too, and Bess was used to them. It was just a surprise added to the close strike of lightning that sent her grabbing the arm of her seat.

Then she felt the soft fast throbbing of the Starlighter's heartbeat as it sped up, faster and faster, pushing away from the storm. "We're good, no damage. That just spooked me a little. I'm not used to storms appearing like that."

"Well," Steve responded, "we're not out of these woods yet."

His comment wasn't just about the great wooded expanse beneath them. Toward the east he could see more dark clouds rolling up the coast. Far ahead, but getting close by the second, was the big open sound, "That's the Croatan Sound," Bess read from her map. "Look for a bridge to the north, that will be just north of the airport."

Steve concentrated on his flying. He could see the storm blowing up from the south as well as behind him. Dark clouds began to blot out the sun in the west, while a long curling front of rain rolled over the southern part of the Outer Banks islands. "I would like to land this thing before we get caught in that big frontal boundary," he said, with a slight worry in his voice. He had flown through rain before, but usually he could fly around or above it. The Starlighter didn't have the range to stay out of the storm for that long.

"We only need a few minutes," Bess countered. She could make out the details of Roanoke Island, their destination, but she hadn't quite spotted the airstrip yet. She looked at her map again, then up through the cupola. "We could go over to the north. Land at the Wright Brothers Monument," she suggested.

"No good," her father exclaimed. "There's no airstrip there. Just a little runway to the south, with too many trees. They're expecting us at Manteo, anyway." All the landing gear and the generator truck would be at the large airstrip just outside the town of Manteo. Bess looked again at her map, glancing over the funny names of the places. One caught her eye. "Wanchese..." she said it out loud, like Wan-cheese, not sure if she was pronouncing it correctly. No place to land there, and by the look of it, already raining on the southern end of the island in that location anyway. "I guess we're just gonna get a little wet," she laughed.

That was the moment the Starlighter crossed from land to flying over the water. "Maybe my joke wasn't too funny," she thought.

She heard a squawk on her radio, which startled her. They had been concentrating on the storm and flying so much they had forgotten that they should call in. A voice came through the static as Steve turned up the volume, "NX4400, this is Dare County Regional Airfield, MQI, you are clear to land at your discretion on the apron of runway 09W."

Steve answered back with a confidence he didn't quite have, "MQI, NX4400, roger."

"Hey, boss, just follow the light, huh?" Bess and Steve recognized the voice of the head of their landing crew, Joel. He had been one of the ranch foremen at their land in Three Winds, the C Bar M, and had come along to run the equipment for landing and takeoffs.

A burst of static, followed by a strange garbled speech came through the radio. At first Bess thought the storm was playing with the sound, but she was sure she heard words. Only she didn't recognize anything that was said in the few seconds she heard them.

Steve was concentrating on getting the Starlighter across the water and to the airport. "Repeat that last, Joel, over," he called.

Joel responded with the same call, "Follow the light. We put on the beacon for you with this rain coming in. It won't be that bad, but I'd like to stay dry if I can, boss. Over."

With that, a bright light appeared to their left and just ahead. It was easy to make out the big airfield now, where both the rotating aerobeacon and a simple white strobe flashed to mark their landing. No time for showing off, Steve thought. He hustled the Starlighter at high speed, threw it into a deep braking manoeuvre, and let the craft dip like a leaf over the big landing pad. When he was sixty feet off the ground, they saw the first sprinkles of rain. Steve expertly tweaked the Starlighter to lean into the wind. It settled down slowly, fighting against the approaching storm.

Steve had to keep the engine up this time, making sure no gusts would send the ship down hard on the tarmac. Agonizingly slowly, he inched the craft down as the winds and rain picked up. But his landing was as gentle as a feather's touch.

Immediately, three men came running out with heavy ropes to tie the craft down to points embedded in the tarmac. They weren't taking chances with the boss and the boss's daughter flying away in a gust of wind.

Bess hopped out of the Starlighter and began to run toward the safety of a nearby hangar. The big front had rolled past, and now the rain came in a steady windy mess. Bess noticed as she ran toward the shelter of the plane hangars that even though the wind blew and rain poured down, it was different from the storms of her home.

"Every time I get out of the Starlighter, I'm in a different place," she thought. Slowing, then stopping in her soaked sneakers, she took in her final landing spot. "I'm already wet," she shrugged, "I might as well look around." The wind was different, all full and powerful, but blustery. It changed direction as it spun her long strawberry blonde hair in different directions. Bess looked out over the water, the sound, to the west, where she had just flown. It was wide and shallow. With the rain coming down in cloudy sheets of mist, she couldn't see to the other side. The water looked like it went on forever.

It was quite a change for a fifteen year old from the open prairie of New Mexico, that was for sure.

After securing the Starlighter in a hangar, Bess climbed into a bright white truck with a logo on the side that said "NACA." It stood for National Advisory Committee on Aeronautics. "NACA has arranged for your housing and transportation," explained the young driver. "They have a house and car available for you at the beach in Nags Head."

Nags Head. Bess laughed softly at the strange name. She realized that many of the places in her home would seem strange to the locals here. Bess decided part of her exploring would be to discover the meanings behind all the funny names on the coast.

They drove through Manteo, on Roanoke Island. As Bess stared out the window, "Look at all these trees!" she cried out. The air was thick, hot, humid. The rain had left everything sticky with the green smell of pine and the rich earthy aroma of rainwater steaming off the asphalt road.

"Over there is The Lost Colony. It's a play about the first English settlers to the New World that came here," explained the driver.

"Why is it called 'The Lost Colony?" Bess asked.

"Because they all disappeared," the driver explained simply. "No one knows what happened to them. A rescue party came back after years away, and they were all gone. Only a word carved on a tree, 'Croatoan', was left to mark where they went."

Bess was fascinated. There certainly was a lot more history here than she had known before.

The big truck chugged its way across the island, then down a long thin road over another marsh, toward a bridge that went over yet another sound. As they cleared the tall trees and got close to the bridge, Bess got a view of the Outer Banks for the first time.

The land stretched out before her, from north to south. It was a thin ribbon of land, dotted with tiny marshy islands that were covered with tall grass. The afternoon light pierced through the clouds, giving an eerie and beautiful look to the land ahead. The darkness of the last remaining clouds darkened the coastal side, while the sound was lit with bright yellow from the sun, and deep green of thick sea grass. The water lapped against the shore in a mix of black and white. Little waves raced to the grass, only to disappear in the marshland. Bess had never seen so much water in her life.

The big truck made it across the bridge to finally bring the Trulys to the end of the world. If Bess had been impressed by the shallow sounds, she was going to be in awe of seeing the Atlantic Ocean for the first time.

The driver took them toward the beach where they turned north to drive up the coast to their house for the week. Tall wide houses dotted sandy hills covered with sharp green grasses that grew like oats. Summer flowers of deep vibrant red grew like weeds straight out of the course yellow sand. There was so much to see, but at the same time, it was so wide open and empty. Low dunes rolled over the land, hiding the great ocean just on the other side. Bess strained in her seat not to jump out to see the ocean.

The driver turned into a long driveway, paved with beach pebbles into a hard concrete that made it look like the very beach had been turned into a paved road. Their vacation beach house was surprisingly big. It had dark wood shingles all over its sides, and a wide covered porch that wrapped around the whole house. The entire building sat on tall pilings that lifted it off the sand.

"Here we are," announced the driver proudly. "This is one of the oldest houses on the Outer Banks. It was one of the first ones built on the shore here in Nags Head."

Bess jumped out, ready to run up to the house and around to the beach side. She hesitated when her father got out to unload their two suitcases.

"Go ahead, kiddo," he said good-naturedly, "I know you want to see the beach."

Bess ran up the steps to the big old house, then around the shaded porch that wrapped around to the back of the beach house.

There it was, the Atlantic Ocean. The ocean stretched out to the horizon, all blue and green water. Waves were just kissing the shore where the receding storm had blown them down to small, foot tall soft rushes of water. All her senses were overloaded with the sights, sounds, and smells of a world she had never felt before. The wind twisted her hair into her face. She smelled so many scents. The ocean threw out a soft salt spray that permeated the air. The sand was wet, with its own strange sickly sweet smell. When the wind blew the tall sea oats and grasses, Bess smelled the wonderful green sweetness of the plants. "Electra would go crazy over all this," Bess thought. Electra, her horse back home, was used to the occasional scrubby plant mixed with her hay. The field of never ending green would probably overwhelm her, Bess thought.

The waves crashed a soft crush on yellow pebbled sand, making a raspy whisper that ran out to a hush as the water washed up and back on the shore. It was a magical sound, regular like a slow ticking clock, but always changing, always a little different. She couldn't wait to get her shoes off and run in the sand.

The back door of the beach house opened, and her driver came out. "I've lived on this island all my life," he said as he, too, admired the view. "I never get tired of this."

Bess could see why. It was comforting. The beach would change, she was sure. It would also always be there. The coast was a strange dynamic place to live, she thought. These people must be comfortable with how things can be different from day to day.

"You'll like this house," he said, turning back to the big old beach house. A large window was salted over with the sea spray, making the view inside, and to the outside, a soft obscured painting, a watercolor of real life.

"One thing you need to know," he went on. "This place has been here for almost a hundred years. A lot of people have been here over that time. A lot of ships were lost just offshore," he said as he pointed to the Atlantic Ocean.

"And a lot of people say that this place is haunted."

CHAPTER 3

Unexpected Guests

Bess was intrigued with the idea of staying in a haunted house. These old homes had so much history to learn. She wasn't really sure there actually were ghosts, but she liked the story. "Really?!" she squealed, "Tell me more!"

"Well," the driver started, "there are lots of legends around here. The former owners say that they would see a shadowy figure, right there," he pointed toward the kitchen door. "But when you look at it, he disappears.

"Now, I don't know about that," the young man spoke with a soft Outer Banks drawl, where he pronounced 'I' as 'Oi'. "But I do know that a lot of these houses were built with whatever they could find. You see, there weren't any lumber yards or wood out here. Everything had to be brought in or found. Supposedly, bits of all these houses are made with wood from shipwrecks all up and down the beach.

When it gets dark, sometimes the ghosts of people walk up and down the beach, like dark shadows, looking for their ships.

"I haven't seen that myself, but my daddy swears he's seen 'em with his own eyes!"

"Great!" Steve Truly came out the back door after hearing the young driver's story, "now she'll never get to sleep!"

"You afraid of ghosts? Sorry," the boy apologized.

"Oh no," Steve responded, "she'll be up all night trying to see one. Bess isn't afraid of anything."

Steve was right. Even with all the travel and work of the day, Bess was up all evening into the late night exploring the house and beach. She had found a book that described how the old houses were built that she read cover to cover, then went around looking for everything she found in the book. Steve found her at 9:00 rolling up the old rug over the wood floor to discover a trap door in the middle of the living room.

"When a storm came, if they couldn't move the house, the owners would evacuate and leave the trap door open. If the house flooded, the water would go in and out this door, so that the house wouldn't float off its pilings!" She thought the design was ingenious.

"Just remember we aren't putting a trap door in back at the ranch!" Steve jokingly insisted.

Bess had gone to sleep late, watching the beach in the darkness from her bedroom in hopes of seeing ghost pirates wandering her shore.

Rising well after the sun, she found her father already with a cup of coffee in his hand, staring out at the risen sun, no longer an orange ball over the horizon, but a white glare on blue water. Sleepily, Bess got a cup for herself. She and Steve fixed toast, eggs, and bacon until the house smelled of all the aromas of breakfast. Bess hurriedly ate. "I want to get out and go swimming, Dad." This would be the first time she had swam in salt water. Bess thought about the times she even had been swimming. Mostly it was just her and her friends splashing in the arroyos back home.

"Alright, kiddo, but only for a little while. We have to go over to the airport right after noon."

Bess ran back to her room to put on her swimsuit. Hawaiian prints were in for the summer, with the exotic island on everyone's mind. This was the first time she had worn her bright red and white suit, festooned with twisted orchids of the tropics.

It was still early enough that the sand hadn't gotten hot. Bess ran barefooted down to the shore. The sand was soft, course, and gave way beneath her feet. Her light steps barely made a dent in the sand as she fairly flew across the shell strewn beach. Her father plodded along happily behind her, swinging an old folding canvas chair behind his shoulder.

There were already other families out, swimming and playing in the shore. Kids floated on inflatables in the wash while a few people swam past the waves into the deeper water to bob up and down, with their heads barely above the ocean.

Bess ran to the water's edge before slowing. The water washed up to her toes and she felt the mild temperature. She shivered with delight at the cold touch that quickly got warmer as she got used to the temperature. The waves were small, but unpredictable. She wasn't sure how to get in. A couple of boys ran to the ocean's edge, charging in and flopping down to their knees as a wave knocked them back. They got up, unfazed, and jumped in like they had done it a hundred times before.

Bess had never done this before.

She waited until a large wave washed up, then quickly walked into the water. The shore dropped out from under her, going to three feet deep in a narrow trough which dropped her into the unexpectedly cool water. She watched the two boys as they sloshed their way straight in past the waves and out into the calm ocean just past the shore break. "That's probably the best idea," Bess thought, and she dove into a rolling wave.

The ocean was wonderful. It was cool until she got used to it, and then felt perfect. The summer sun kept her warm as she swam and splashed through the waves. She floated on her back, which she found to be very easy in the salt water. The ocean was all real and natural and different. She watched as hundreds of tiny shining fish jumped out of her way when she swam through their miniature school. Long thin ribbons of sea grass caught in her hands and toes. The sand under the water was strangely firm. It wasn't muddy at all, she realized.

Swimming in the ocean allowed her to stretch her body in ways she hadn't been able to do when she was flying for the past days. Her shoulders and legs moved freely, twisting out the knots of sitting and waiting. "I could do this all day. Every day," she thought. She lay on her back, her hair flowing out like a net in the water. Bess imagined catching the tiny fish in her hair, while the seaweed dangled into bows, until she turned into a mermaid and swam out to sea.

With her face barely above water, she could only hear the soft deep rush of waves as they ran to the shore. Another sound came to her, a deep soft rumble, much farther, very low, a drum beat in slow motion. Then she heard a higher call from above the water.

Bess kicked herself upright and stood in the water as she shook her hair out of her face. Her father was calling her name from the beach, and touching his wristwatch. "Time to go," he was telling her.

It was with a slightly sad heart that Bess left the beach to shower and change. They drove back toward the airport in Manteo in a big Buick convertible that was on loan to them. "We're VIPs," Steve explained.

NACA had arranged for a car for them, along with an old Willys Jeep that was parked in the old carriage shed near the road. The house belonged to a pilot who lived up in Virginia, and it had been arranged for Steve to use the place and the Jeep while they were down.

"What are we doing at the airport, Dad?" Bess asked as she waved her hand up and down in the wind as the big Buick rolled like a blue and white wave over the road.

"Well, we have to make some plans to fly the Starlighter over to the monument tomorrow," Steve started to go over his list of to-do's. "There's no airstrip there, so we have to find a place to land it. And I know a couple people who are flying in today. I want to see them.

"Plus, I have a surprise for you," Steve said mysteriously.

As they drove up to the airport on the far end of Roanoke Island, Bess saw the air full of planes, with more taxiing or parked on the tarmac. There were several of the new Cessna Skyhawks, sleek little planes with covered landing wheels. A larger two engined Twin Bonanza churned its propellers as it made its way to a parking spot near the water. Bess reached over to tap the steering wheel as her father drove. "Pay attention to the road til we get there, Daddy-O," she teased. Her father was in heaven with all the planes.

Steve already had a smile on his face. Bess's comment only made his white teeth gleam brighter.

And no surprise. Steve was a star there. He and Bess pulled up to their hangar in a big blue and white convertible, next to a gleaming chrome airship sitting on the tarmac. Even in the summer heat, Steve slipped on his old flight jacket as he stepped out of the car. Pilots, ground crew, and many of the locals all stopped to see the man as he walked toward the Starlighter.

Bess walked away, leaving her father to all the stardom that came with being a hotshot pilot with a fast aircraft. It was Saturday, and a lot of kids and teenagers were out near the airport, watching the planes land. She was naturally drawn toward the water at the edge of the runway. It was yet another noticeable difference from her home. Here planes came in for landings over a wide body of water. At the edge, she saw kids splashing in the shallow sound. Bess walked over to an old dock nearby, where some kids and teens hopped into the water. She slipped off her shoes and walked out in her shorts.

The water felt different to her. The sand was all muddy and silty, with a strange marshy smell. It was warm, almost uncomfortably so. The local kids didn't seem to mind, though.

"It barely gets deeper than this," one boy, about eleven years old, said as he splashed up to Bess on the shore. "You could walk out for a mile and not get your arms wet."

"Really?" Bess couldn't imagine a body of water that wide also being that shallow.

"Yeah!" exclaimed a girl who had followed the boy, "but where's the fun in that?" And she stuck her hands into the water with a big *swoosh* to splash the boy mercilessly, who happily splashed her back. The two ran off through the shallows, their legs pumping against the water as they jumped and stomped their way through a very wet game of chase.

Bess walked back to the earthy shore while she wiped the water off her face from the kids' game. It tasted funny, not salty like the ocean. "Pff... I kissed a frog!" she exclaimed.

"Sorry about that," a towel appeared next to her, attached to an arm. "Those two, this is the only place I can slow them down."

Bess looked past the towel to find a young girl's smiling face. "You gotta know yer gonna get wet comin' out here. Hi, I'm Vicki Tillett. You must be here from one of those planes, huh?"

"Yes," said Bess, "Hi, Vicki, I'm Bess Truly. Yeah, I flew in with my father. He's been wanting to come here for years. He's a pilot." Bess left off the part where she, too, was a pilot. She had spent so much of the trip explaining the Starlighter that she wanted to, for a little while, just be a teenager.

Bess and Vicki were able to talk for a few minutes. They were often interrupted with cries of the kids trying to get Vicki to come swimming with them, or airplanes landing overhead. Vicki occasionally babysat the kids, and had come over with their parents to let them swim while they watched the planes land.

"I'm staying in Nags Head, at one of those old brown houses on the beach. It's supposed to be..." Bess looked to make sure the kids weren't near, "haunted."

Vicki laughed at Bess being so secretive. "All those places are haunted. There are so many ghost stories around here, you wouldn't believe it."

Bess told Vicki where she was staying, and it turned out that Vicki lived nearby, on the other side of the beach, in the maritime forest on the sound side. They had just mentioned their mutual love of horses, when Bess heard her name being called. Her father had come to find her.

"Hey, it was nice to meet ya," Vicki said.

"Yeah, maybe I'll see you over at the beach this week. Bye!"

Steve waved for Bess to hurry. "I'm sorry to take you away from your friend there, but I have a surprise for you. Come on, kiddo. You're going to want to see this."

The two hurried back to their spot by the Starlighter. A large crowd had gathered around the craft, and ropes had been set up to keep the visitors away from the edge of the airplane. Most of them had stopped looking and were now scanning the sky.

Around the hangars were temporary speakers that carried the control room radio, announcing planes that were landing moment by moment. At this moment, nothing was landing. Everyone was waiting.

Finally, far to the north, a loud growl came out of the sky. At high speed a plane came out of the clear blue. It was thin and fast, "definitely a prop plane," Bess could tell by the noise, but much faster and louder than the usual civilian planes that had landed so far.

It came across the sky, over the sound, where it turned into a wide bank. The plane finally showed more than its silhouette. It was a bright shiny chrome that glinted in the midday sun that first showed the shape of the craft. Many pilots oooh'ed appreciatively. "What is that, Dad?" Bess asked. She recognized the shape, but also didn't. It was a familiar shape that had been changed enough that she didn't know it.

"It's an F-82, a Twin Lightning."

The big plane was a version of the old fighter plane that Steve had flown long ago. It had two engines and two cockpits. "NACA used this one as a test for rockets a few years ago. They flew it in as a showpiece."

And to the pilots it was. Even though the plane was older, it was unique. As it taxied to a stop, visitors crowded nearby, waiting for the propeller to stop spinning. Bess started to walk over, but Steve held her back.

"Wait, that's not the surprise."

No one noticed the next plane coming in. It was a less exciting craft, a simple Beechwood Bonanza, with a split V tail making it easy to recognize. The plane landed and taxied over to a spot next to the Starlighter.

When the propeller stopped spinning, the door opened. Bess was stunned when she saw who got out.

CHAPTER 4

Ghosts In The Mists

Two girls piled out of the double doors of the little plane, squealing with delight at seeing their friend Bess. Aurora Baca and Lydia Lanier raced out of the plane, screaming her name. Bess ran forward to hug her two best friends. Behind them, Jesse Armstrong pushed a seat forward to get out of the back, while the copilot's door opened over the wing and a striking woman in black sunglasses climbed gracefully out onto the wing and hopped down.

"Mom?!" Bess was surprised to see her friends, but she definitely had no idea that her mother was coming across the country, too.

"There is no way I would miss a trip to the beach, dear," said Portia Truly, then she smiled with bright white teeth over her bright red lipstick. Her red-brown hair blew away from her as she stepped away from the plane. She looked like a movie star arriving at an awards show, Bess thought.

She really was a star here, Bess then realized. She was the one who designed the engine for the Starlighter. The aircraft and Portia Truly had the same heart. That beat that Bess heard regularly was part of her mother.

Portia Truly was a nuclear physicist and engineer. She had designed both the electric propulsion for the Starlighter as well as her static discharge device. Bess had affectionately nicknamed it the Zap-Gun. It could put out a bright blue light day or night, and at higher settings could send a powerful blue spark of static electricity that could dig holes in the dirt or melt metal together. Bess had used it regularly in her work at the ranch, as well as on rare occasions for more important and desperate occasions. Her friends Lydia and Aurora also used them, and her father had given them the nickname The Zap-Gun Rangers when they rode around the prairie on horseback.

Hugging her mom, Bess then went to help Jesse load up the car with the light luggage from the Bonanza.

"You're going to love this place," Bess exclaimed to Jesse as he admired the big car. Jesse loved cars and anything mechanical. A year older, Jesse had his drivers license and had often given the girls a ride to their next adventure in his orange dune buggy. The big Buick was a level of magnitude higher in his world.

"I already do," he said back, putting his arms out to take in the gigantic convertible. "You think your dad will let me drive?"

Bess laughed. Her father had always expressed a complete confidence in Jesse's ability to do any task, including getting Bess and her girlfriends out of trouble.

The family and friends were able to pile into the big car, with Steve driving, Bess in the middle and her mother leaning over the passenger side, while Jesse, Aurora, and Lydia rode in the back. Bess was constantly twisting in her seat, trying to tell both her mother in the front and her friends in the back all the stories she had learned.

"And the water is cool, but it warms up, and it's full of fish! Little fish, it's okay, and seaweed," Lydia made a face, "no, it's fine, and guess what? Our house is *HAUNTED*! And there's a trap door that..."

"Wait, slow down," Jesse spoke up first, as Aurora stared open mouthed, "What's up with this ghost?"

"It's not haunted," Steve reassured them. "All the houses down here, they have legends attached to them. There were shipwrecks here for hundreds of years. The ocean here is called The Graveyard Of The Atlantic because of all the ships that sank here. The government built several lighthouses on the coast because of it. We'll go see a couple." He attempted to get the conversation back on a more earthly track.

"Bess, sit still," Portia requested. "I've been moving up and down for an hour. Let me be level for a few moments."

Bess smiled at her mom, then immediately turned around and said, "I'll tell you all about it on the beach when we get there."

Bess hurried her friends through the house when they got to the home. Jesse tried to look around at the place. "So who owns this?" he asked as he looked at a big radio on a table.

"It belongs to a pilot friend of mine. He flies down here from outside of Washington, DC. He likes to listen to the planes and boats talk," explained Steve.

"Jesse, hurry up," pleaded Aurora, " I want to get to the beach!"

The four of them changed and ran out to the shore. Bess watched her friends experience the sand and ocean for the first time just like her. Aurora ran fast, her sandals flopping up sand as her cover up flared out behind her. Lydia held onto her hat, wanting to run like Aurora toward the shore, but protecting her looks and dignity as she strolled through the soft sand. Jesse crested the low sand dune and stopped. He took in the fullness of the view, how the ocean stretched from end to end, as far as the eye can see. He took a deep breath of the fresh salt air. Then he tore off after the girls, catching and outracing them until he plowed gracelessly into the low waves where he flopped into the water. Jesse popped up, shaking his hair, then dove back under water and began swimming.

Bess understood all their feelings. It was exactly what she felt only a day ago, and even just hours. She walked down the beach where she threw down a towel and then strolled to the shore break. "You just have to jump in!" she told her friends, "Jesse's got the right idea."

"But it's cold!" Lydia cried, with her arms up as she tiptoed her way into deeper water.

"Go on, get your hair wet, Lydia," chided Aurora. She pinched her nose, counted inwardly, squeezed her eyes shut and ducked under the water. Seconds later, she came back up, her long raven black hair no longer full but slick running down the back of her head. "Oh, that's great!"

"Here goes nothing," Lydia said with some apprehension. She leaned forward, water going up to her neck, then threw her arms out and dove into an approaching wave. Lydia may have been afraid of the cold water, but once in she swam like a fish, coming up twenty seconds later farther out from where she started. "Ooo, that does feel nice. Better than any old arroyo anytime." The girls were used to splashing around in the shallow river near their homes, not swimming in deep salt water.

Bess joined her friends in the ocean, and the four of them swam throughout the rest of the day. Jesse discovered he could swim out into the water where it was so deep he couldn't dive down to touch the bottom. The girls joined him, all four floating on their backs with their eyes closed, seeing the afternoon sun shine through their lids. It was a peaceful moment that stretched into an afternoon.

"I could do this forever," breathed Lydia as she slowly stroked her arms through the calm ocean. The water had turned a deep green as the sun began to lower over the dunes.

"I thought the same thing," Bess answered. "Can you imagine, a never ending summer, every day, chasing the sun, swimming, suntans, nights in a hammock..."

"Eating seafood," added Aurora. Her swimming had really built up an appetite.

"Yeah, my stomach is rumbling," said Jesse.

"Mine, too," added Bess. "Hey, that's not my stomach." She felt a strange ripple go through her body. A deep low quiver seemed to shake her, as if a big truck was going by. Only there was no road out in the ocean. "Do you feel that? Wait, ... do you hear something?"

She dove under water, her eyes closed, listening. A low hum came through the water, deep, like a rolling bass drum. The others dove into the water, too.

When they popped back up, Bess spit, squinted water out of her eyes, and spoke, "You heard that, too?"

"Yes," Lydia said. "I think Jesse is so hungry he's making *my* stomach growl!"

"That's not my stomach," Jesse insisted, then splashed at Lydia. "Maybe it's a boat far out to sea."

"Maybe it's a sea monster!" said Aurora.

"Maybe it's Bess's ghost!" added Lydia.

Bess smiled at all the teasing, how her friends could keep up with each other. Being at the coast and far away from home was a great adventure, but she was happier to have friends to share in it.

It almost made her forget the strange sound they heard.

Right up until it stopped.

"It's not there anymore," she said. "Weird."

Aurora looked around, as if she could see the source somehow. "Yeah... I guess that is the word for it. Weird."

"Let's get out and go have a snack," Jesse decided to change the subject.

Back at the beach house, the four kids stood on the back porch, towels wrapped around them, as they all ate snacks. It was 4:00, which was a difficult time of day for the New Mexico group. It was too early for dinner, but past the time they usually ate lunch back home, and all the kids were hungry from swimming.

"Why don't you shower off and I'll start cooking," suggested Steve. "We are going to try a local delicacy, fried shrimp."

Aurora, always hungry, and Jesse, ready to try any food from another place, both agreed readily. Lydia was less sure about eating shrimp that was not a cocktail. Bess knew her father was a great cook, and she would enjoy anything he made.

"Look!" Jesse called out, "They have a shower outside!" A small room, really just four sheets of plywood nailed to posts, with one hinged as a door, hid a simple pipe and shower head. Jesse ran down to it and turned the water on. "Oh, man, I gotta try this!"

The kids took turns in the showers in and outside the house. Lydia couldn't bring herself to shower outside, while Aurora didn't want to get out. "This water tastes great," she commented. The house used well water, cold and mineral tasting, to wash off the salt water that dried to an itchy scale on everyone and everything.

The household had an early dinner of batter fried shrimp that smelled up the house with the scent of deep fried food, mixed with the wonderful salt air, along with a large bag of frozen french fries cooked in the oven, and bottles of Coke that quickly became wet and dewy in the late summer heat. Jesse especially liked the fried shrimp, and even Lydia complimented the taste of fresh seafood, as well as the cooking of Bess's father.

"He is an outstanding cook," Portia agreed as she got up with her empty plate, kissing her husband on the head as she walked to the kitchen.

"Here, honey, I'll take that," Steve tried to take the plate, but Portia had nothing with that.

"The cook shouldn't clean," she said. Jesse and Bess agreed. They quickly gathered up the rest of the plates and ran into the kitchen to wash them.

The evening came on quickly. The kids sat on the back porch, satisfied with their dinner, rocking peacefully in chairs to a regular squeaking from the old wooden floor. Bess had shown her friends the hidden trap door which lead to the sandy ground under the house. Cold air, never warmed by sun, came up in a whiff, strangely dry and wooden smelling. "Great for sneaking out," said Aurora.

"To where?" asked Jesse. Not far off to the west was the giant set of sand dunes called Jockey's Ridge. Beyond that was a maritime forest full of trees. That looked like where all the ghosts would be, not in this place, Jesse thought.

"To the beach!" insisted Aurora. She ran out the back door, down the old wooden walkway, and out into the sand. Lydia looked at the others, shrugged, and took off, with Bess and Jesse on her heels.

It was late now, with the sun setting in the west that created a fiery orange and purple sky. A haze blew in from far offshore. The waves were being topped by a light breeze which licked the salt out of the ocean and sent it into the air. To the north and south, white lights that turned on at two fishing piers began to twinkle and hide in the darkening mist.

"Now, *this* looks like a time for the ghosts to come out," said Aurora. Stars were twinkling on over the ocean horizon, and far away, lights blinked from a ship passing far off in the Atlantic.

"That noise sure was strange, that thing we heard," Bess said as she thought about the day she had. "I don't hear it now."

The others stopped to listen. Only the soft rush of low waves came quietly over the beach. They heard no other sounds.

Bess turned to face the beach as it went north, into the salty mist. She imagined ghost pirates rowing in from a cursed ship, intent on burying their treasure. She could almost see the ghosts of all those shipwrecked travelers and sailors in the darkening red sky.

Then suddenly, she saw a dark form start to appear in the mist. A strange sound came from the distance, as the shape got larger, more distinct.

"Oh my goodness!" Bess cried out. "Look at that!"

CHAPTER 5

Shark Bait

Out of the mists came a huge dark shadow, slowly plodding toward Bess and her friends. Once it got close enough, Bess recognized the shape as that of a large black horse, with a rider on it riding bareback. The horse trotted slowly up toward the kids and stopped.

"Hi," said the rider. Bess looked up, first admiring the beautiful black mare before looking at the rider. She recognized the girl on the horse. "Vicki? Is that you? It's me, Bess Truly, we met over at the airport!"

"Bess! Hi, I was hoping I would see you out on the beach. I got a late start on my ride, as you can see." She waved her arm up at the setting sun.

Bess introduced her friends to Vicki. The local girl had a home on the other side of Jockey's Ridge, and rode to the beach often in the summer. Her family had several horses in a small farm over in the woods nearby. "You'll have to come over sometime. Nags Head Woods is a great place to ride and explore," she said.

It was getting dark, and Vicki needed to get her horse home before it got too late. "It gets dark late in the summer, but it gets real dark real quick here," she said.

The next day, Vicki met Bess and her friends on the beach where they spent the morning swimming. Vicki filled them in on some of the legends of the islands that were her home. "Oh, yeah," she exclaimed, "my granddaddy would tell me stories of ghosts in every house, and behind every tree back in Nags Head Woods. Scared me to death. We thought he was just trying to frighten us, but he believes every story he tells.

"That big dune over there, Jockey's Ridge? That's where Nags Head got its name. Long time ago, the people that lived back there would tie a candle lamp on an old horse and walk it up and down the dune at night. Sailing captains would see it and think it was ship in a harbor. They would sail in, crash their ship on the sandbars out here," she gestured to the water all around them, "and the land pirates would come out and take everything, kill the crew, and strip the boats of all the wood. The place was named after the old nag with a lamp around its head. Yeah, a lot of these houses probably have shipwreck parts hidden somewhere on them.”

Jesse was in awe, fascinated with the story. But Aurora questioned it. “Wait, no way an old horse would let someone put a burning candle under their neck!”

“Yes!” Vicki agreed, “Finally, someone else who said the same thing I did! I don’t believe that story either. But I’ll tell ya this, over there a ways, there’s these seven dunes, and at night, a light appears floating over the dunes. No one knows what it is. But I seen it with my own eyes!” She made a big googly eyed face in emphasis.

“I got some ghost books I can loan you if you like. Lots of stories around here,” she offered.

When they were out swimming, Aurora saw some dorsal fins appear about a hundred yards offshore. The big black fins popped up and rolled into the water where they disappeared and reappeared farther down the water. “Are those... sharks?” she asked Vicki.

“No, don’t worry, those are porpoises. Like a dolphin.”

“Do you have sharks around here?” Jesse asked. He thought it would be cool to see a shark. From a distance.

“Oh yeah, sure, little ones, mostly. They won’t hurt you. Sandbar sharks, blacktips, they’re about four feet long, they like the shipwrecks around here. We get a few hammerheads. Mean, ugly dudes. But they all mostly stay offshore, especially now. I've never seen a shark in the shallow water around here. Too cold, I think. But hey, if the water is salty, somewhere there's a shark in it. It's their home, not ours."

It was a very thoughtful comment that Vicki made. Bess came to vacation on the Outer Banks, a place where very few people had ever moved by accident, except for the original shipwreck survivors that Vicki had told them about. The sharks were natives to the ocean.

"Hey, how about you meet me this afternoon over at the Sea Breeze Pier?" she pointed just south. It's closer than the Nags Head Fishing Pier," she jerked her thumb over her shoulder to the long pier to their north. "I can show you how to catch some fish for dinner."

"Sounds keen," Bess said.

Vicki headed home to take care of her horse, promising to meet up at the pier. The rest of the group went inside for lunch. Steve was sitting on the back porch, reading a book and listening to the big radio that broadcast local plane chatter. Somehow he understood the talk through the static. Bess noticed how the regular talk would fade out to a hazy wave of nothing but static. It sounded a lot like the waves on the shore, only unrelenting. Then, hidden in the static, she heard someone talking, only to fade away.

"What was that? I thought I heard something like that when we were landing the Starlighter. It sounds like someone talking, but I don't understand them."

"I heard that, too," Portia said as she came in with a cold glass of iced tea. "I would think it was someone on a nearby frequency interfering with this one, or perhaps a ship passing by. It's strange that it fades in and out. The broadcaster must be far away."

Strange and stranger, Bess thought. "This is a different world from home."

That afternoon Jesse drove the girls down to the pier, where they met Vicki and a few of her friends. They were able to rent poles and buy bait to go out on the pier for their first salt water fishing lesson. The pier was yet another unique and different spot for the four of them. It was a long wooden structure that stuck out over 700 feet into deep water. The pilings and walkway were all built of creosoted wood, soaked with oil to keep the wood from rotting in the ocean. Bess could feel the waves underneath them as they moved the pier slightly. Aurora walked down the middle. Normally brave and curious, she was not in her element on the pier. Jesse stared over the edge at the water below. He expected to see schools of fish swarming around the lures, but the clear water was deep, hiding all the creatures in its depths until a lucky angler pulled a catch up to the pier railing.

Vicki helped them bait hooks and cast. Bess was used to fishing in the rivers, but the surf rods and reels were much larger and heavier. And the smells were all different. The sea smell mixed with the creosote pier and the scent of fresh fish that was caught and thrown into buckets for anglers to clean and take home for dinner or the freezer. "That's a sheepshead, good eatin' but a little bony," she explained as Aurora caught her first fish, a beautiful black and white striped fish. "Trout, that's a tasty fish. We catch lots of them," she said of another catch.

Lydia squealed when a fisherman nearby her pulled up a long silver ribbonfish. The four foot long fish was shiny with a set of pointy sharp teeth. The fish looked terrifying as it wiggled like a snake. "That was in the water?!" she cried.

"Aw, don't worry," the old fisherman laughed. He stepped on the fish as he pulled out the hook. "Look at that mouth!" He held up the fish so the crowd around him could see it. "He's got those sharp bony teeth so he can grab little fish and hold on to them." He waved it at Lydia, who shrank back. "He wouldn't want to eat you. You won't fit in his mouth!"

Bess laughed as the man tossed the ribbonfish back. It sailed down in a twisting dive before cutting through the water and swimming away.

Bess was standing idly, holding her rod against the railing where notches had been worn from so many years of fishing poles leaning there. Suddenly, the line jerked and popped. She grabbed the reel quickly and pulled to set the hook. Whatever she caught, it sure felt big.

"It could be anything," shouted Lydia.

"It could be a shark," commented Jesse hopefully.

"It could be a skate," said Vicki.

Bess wondered how someone would catch a roller skate in the ocean. Maybe it was like catching a shoe in a lake.

But it was none of those. With a little help and a lot of encouragement, Bess reeled in a big fish. Big to her at least. It was long, silver, with a bright green top and spiky fins going down to a thin tail. Vicki grabbed her line and heaved the fish over the rail to the pier. "That's a Spanish Mackerel."

"Like 'Holy Mackerel?'" Jesse said.

"Better," replied Vicki. "You can eat this."

Bess enjoyed her celebrity with the big catch. Vicki threw it into a big bucket with a few other fish, including Aurora's sheepshead. "I'll clean these for you. Show you how to filet them and we'll put them on ice, but you oughta..."

A yell permeated the air, from the end of the pier. Bess looked down the walkway to see a fisherman fall backwards as a fish flew up to the pier attached to his line. Or at least a piece of a fish. The big catch had been cleanly bitten below the head. The slight curve showed that it had been bitten clean off.

"A shark got my catch!" he yelled as he rubbed his head where he hit it.

Everyone ran to the end of the pier to look for the shark. Depending upon their wishes, they were either not disappointed, or terrified.

The ocean was full of sharks churning up the water with their fins and tails. They were in a frenzy as they swarmed all the fish around the pier.

CHAPTER 6

A Quick Swim

The yelling started first. Then there was the screaming.

Bess saw the sharks circling madly, as they got closer and closer to the shore. Everyone else on the pier was transfixed by the mad aquatic show. Even their friend Vicki softly commented, "I've never seen anything like this before."

Some fishermen on the pier were trying to yell down to the beach to warn the swimmers, but their voices carried poorly in the wind from so far away. Bess dropped her pole and began running.

She made it through the pier house on the beach and jumped the railing to the soft sand underneath. That's when she heard the first scream of terror.

The swimmers had seen the sharks, along with hundreds of other jumping fish, all swarming into a frenzy as they closed in on the shallow shore. A mother was running into the waves after her children who stood out on an underwater sandbar. The waves pushed her back as she tried to walk out to get her kids.

"She doesn't know how to swim!" Bess ran past her and dove in, cutting through the waves with outstretched arms. She came up through the wave and began pulling with her arms in a powerful freestyle stroke. The salt water stung her eyes, but she kept them open to see where she was going. It was only twenty feet out, she guessed, but the waves were rolling in deep from the sandbar, making her swimming difficult.

With every breath, she heard more yelling, more screaming. Bess didn't know how close the sharks were, but she knew she had to help get those kids in. She felt her hand scrape the bottom. The sandbar came up quickly to meet her.

Bess stood up, struggling against the waves and soft sand. A rolling wave nearly knocked her back, but she pushed through it with her shoulder. Lifting her feet out of the shallow water, Bess ran toward the two kids, who were unaware of what the danger was, only that people were screaming.

The sandbar was shallow, only two or three feet deep. Bess hoped it was too shallow for a shark. She looked at the kids and saw the confused look in their faces, with a small mix of panic. Reflexively, Bess looked past them into the deeper ocean. Just outside the approaching waves she saw the fins slashing through the water. The kids followed her gaze as they saw the look of fear on her face. When they saw the sharks' fins, they screamed and tried to struggle toward Bess and the safety of shore.

Bess splashed toward them with her arms open, but always with an eye to the sea. The next wave rolled over the end of the sandbar and broke. She could see in it schools of fish, all caught in the wash as they swam from the bigger predators. The fish scattered north and south as the wave broke.

Gathering the two little kids, Bess hurried them toward the deep trough that separated the sandbar from the shore. "C'mon, it's alright, I got you," she assured them. Bess wondered how believable she sounded.

Scooping them up in one arm as best as she could, Bess prepared to swim the two back to shore. With a final glance over her shoulder, she saw the next wave break. This one was bigger, and in it she could easily make out the shape of a much larger fish.

A shark.

It tumbled in the wave until it found the bottom of the soft sandbar. Bess saw its tail thrash to get purchase and send it back out to sea. She worried it would swim toward any deep water, and the nearest deep water was right in front of her.

"Let's hope this is one of those sharks that has a small mouth," Bess thought as she remembered the fisherman's words.

Bess dove into the water with the two kids clutched closely to her. With one arm, she stroked toward the shore, kicking her legs like scissors in a fast side stroke.

"Hold your breath!" she burbled. The big wave had caught up to them. The kids and her were going under. She hoped it was only a wave that came up to her. She may be bigger than a shark, but her feet, and the kids' feet, would probably fit in the mouth of that one she just saw.

Under the wave, she still swam forward as hard as she could. For a terrified moment, she felt something soft, but very firm, brush up against her ankle. She kicked at it hard and screamed under the water before popping up, coughing and gurgling. She couldn't help herself. She looked back to make sure she still had a foot.

No blood, she noticed, no pain, but a lot of fear. Bess began swimming hard again. Within two strokes she felt something reach out and take the kids from her. Looking up, she saw Jesse standing chest deep in the water with his clothes soaked. Lydia and Aurora stood behind him.

"Come on, get out," Lydia was waist deep in the water even though she was wearing jeans and a summer top. When it came down to helping her friends, fashion didn't matter to her. She helped pull an exhausted Bess from the water.

"I guess I didn't have to worry..." she panted, tired but happy to have gotten the kids to safety. Maybe there wasn't any danger from sharks in water that shallow, she thought before glancing back out to the ocean.

At that moment, all of them saw a tall sharp fin and thrashing tail, right where Bess and the kids had been. A huge hammerhead struggled to find its way back out to sea.

It was a wet and sullen ride back to the beach house for Bess. Jesse and Aurora tried to put a good face on the events. "Hey, I wanted to see a shark!" Jesse joked. Lydia took her top off and sunned herself in her bathing suit in the back seat of the old Jeep, trailing her summer shirt by the straps in the wind to dry it. Bess brooded. "That certainly was a strange event. I don't know much about sharks, but I don't think they normally do that."

After changing and filling in her father on the events at the pier, he had a suggestion. "I'm going to a marina later today. I wanted to see if I could charter a fishing boat. Let's go down there and see if anyone knows about what happened."

Bess and Aurora rode with Steve down to the marina at Oregon Inlet. The marina was named after the big cut in the island just south of it. In 1846, a hurricane had lashed the Outer Banks. It cut a hole in the thin islands, and a sailing ship, the *Oregon*, sailed in to ride out the storm in the calmer and more protective sound. The opening provided an easy access to sport fishermen in boats with long sharp bows to go out in the Gulf Stream to catch game fish. Blue marlin were a popular trophy fish to go after, while other visitors went fishing for fish to eat, like mackerel or pompano, or a shiny fast tuna.

When they parked and got out, Bess was inundated with familiar and new sights and smells. The boats were long, low, white, with big tall bridges for spotting fish. Outrigger poles stretched out to the sides, giving the sleek boats spindly arms. The place reeked of all types of pungent smells. Creosote from the docks, diesel for the boats, salt and sea life from the fish being unloaded off a boat that had recently arrived. The whole marina was new. It had a sparkling view out into the sound and the lowering afternoon sun, and the not far off exit of Oregon Inlet into the Atlantic Ocean and Gulf Stream beyond. In the distance, a ferry steamed cars over to Hatteras Island and the villages to the south.

Steve walked up to a couple of people he recognized as fellow pilots, while Bess and Aurora looked at the fish being unload from a recent catch.

"What are those?" Aurora asked, pointing at a remarkable fish of green and yellow. It had a sleek body with a tall flat head. "They're incredible looking!"

"Them's dolphin," said a teenage boy throwing fish after fish out of an icy storage hold.

"Dolphin?" Aurora was confused. The didn't look like the big cute dolphin she had seen in pictures. "You caught baby dolphin?! You're going to eat them?"

"Naow," said the boy, laughing at the tourist, "They're dolphin *fish*, loike a pompano, not dolphin *mammal*, loike a whale." The rough teenager was obviously a local, letting his accent fly as he hurriedly displayed his charter's daily catch.

Bess didn't know what a dolphin fish was, or a pompano, but she guessed they were types of fish caught around the beach.

Behind them, a voice spoke up. "Dolphin, the fish," a young woman pointed at the shiny green fish, "is named that because they swim in front of boats, like a dolphin. They are a plentiful fish. They are popular eating fish, and very tasty. Some people call it a dorado, or a mahi mahi in Hawaii. I call it a Coryphaena hippurus.

"But only around other ichthyologists," she smiled at her own joke. "Hi, I'm Jamie Hodgson. I'm a fish scientist. I'm studying the fish and how they grow here on the Outer Banks."

Bess introduced herself. "I'm Bess Truly. This is my friend Aurora Baca. We're here with my father. We flew in for Aviation Day."

"Hey," inquired Aurora, "since you're an ickyologist," she had never heard the term before, "do you know anything about sharks? We had the strangest thing happen to us today."

Bess and Aurora explained the events that led up to their close call with a shark. Jamie listened intently, but she had a look on her face like she didn't fully believe the two teens. "That certainly isn't typical behavior for sharks. A single one might come close to shore hunting for food, but you wouldn't have that many show up in the shallows all at one time. Possibly a few sandbar sharks..." she suggested.

Bess was distracted by her father waving to her. He was standing with a few other men looking at their catch that was just taken off one of the big offshore fishing yachts, while yet another big boat, white, sleek and long, cruised in toward the slip next to them. "Bess, this Captain Tommy Tillett. He's going to take me out fishing the day after tomorrow. You want to see the boat?"

"Tillett? We met a girl named Vicki Tillett. Are you related to her?"

Captain Tillett laughed, "We're all related, somehow. We got Tilletts here like most cities got Smiths!"

His good natured laughing was cut short as the white boat pulled in hurriedly to its slip. The boy working as a mate was trying to tie the boat up to a piling, but the two men who had chartered it, notably different in dress and lack of tan to the captain and the young mate, were in a desperate act to jump off the boat.

"No way!" One yelled as he ran off the little dock toward the sandy soil behind the marina's bulkhead. "Never again!"

The other man likewise jumped off. He, too, seemed shook, almost terrified, at the thought of spending another second on the boat.

The captain quickly jumped off, but did not pursue the two men.

"What happened?" asked Captain Tillett. "What's wrong with them two?"

"I don't blame 'em," the other captain said. On the boat, the young mate just shook his head. "We were out fishin' for marlin, hooked a good one, too." He was exasperated, as if he could hardly believe the words he was to say. "We lost it. The whole thing, I swear, no one's gonna believe it, but the whole fish was bitten off...

"by a sea monster!"

CHAPTER 7

Danger On The Horizon

Bess expected there to be a big group of fishermen chortling and then laughing at the captain, but to her surprise, all the fishing boat captains seemed to stop what they were doing and come over to hear more. Only did a few of the tourists and clients chuckle at the idea.

Bess, Aurora, and Steve looked at each other knowingly. They had seen things before that people would just as easily classify as unbelievable, so they knew not to doubt someone immediately.

"What do you mean, 'sea monster'? What did you see?" asked Captain Tillett.

"We had just hooked this big marlin, a huge blue, musta been ten, twelve feet. We saw it jump, it was on the line, set," the captain even made a hook shape with his fingers for emphasis. "One big jump, then we saw this thing..." he just shook his head.

"It tore up the water, tore the whole ocean up behind the fish. Just came up behind and took the whole dang thing!"

"What did it look like?" this time Jamie, the ichthyologist, chimed in. She seemed like she was more on the doubting side.

"We didn't see it," exclaimed the mate from the back of the boat. "It was under water, just cutting below the surface. I swear I saw a fin, but it was like glass or somethin'," he shook his head. Even the poor kid couldn't believe his own tale. "But we *saw* it. It was there, a big dark shape, like a tube of water. It must have been sixty feet long!"

"Impossible," half whispered Jamie. "Maybe it was a whale, or a submarine?" even her words seemed hollow, as she tried to recreate the story into something she could believe.

"Impossible, huh?" the captain became his old salt self. "Snapped right through this leader?!" he angrily waved a frayed thick wire and tangled monofilament line. "We were there, saw it happen." he waved at the rapidly disappearing clients, now in their car and driving away. "Scare those two near to death?"

"It weren't no submarine, neither," said the mate. "I seen it. Loike I said, it tore that water up. It twisted in the water, it bent. I seen whales before, I known what they look like. Weren't no whale, weren't no submarine."

"Where did this happen?" asked Steve. He glanced at Bess nervously.

"'Bout twelve, fifteen miles out. Off of Nags Head, up north a ways. Out near where them big herring trawlers go, the international boats." Twelve miles offshore the waters were no longer US controlled, and often international fisheries came to catch herring or mackerel.

The ride back to their beach house was first full of questions. The girls wondered if the event had anything to do with the sharks they saw onshore. They had discussed only a little with the scientist they had met. Bess had invited her to see the Starlighter fly tomorrow, and she hoped to see the woman again and discuss her work.

Soon, the girls realized they had more questions than answers. The talk in the car got quiet. Bess and Aurora leaned their hands out the side of the convertible, each cutting through the air like a shark's fin slicing the water.

The next day Bess arose early. It was Aviation Day, and she and her father were going over to the airport to fly the Starlighter over to the Wright Brothers Monument. Aurora and Lydia slept in, while Bess, her parents, and Jesse arose to have an early breakfast of bacon, eggs, toast, and coffee. The plans of the busy day took the place of all the strange events of yesterday afternoon. The Starlighter would be fully charged for a short flight from the airport to a landing pad installed at the Wright Brothers Monument. Jesse would drive Bess and Steve to the Starlighter, while Portia took the girls over to the monument later that morning.

At the airport, most of the preparation had already been done. The Starlighter was ready for launch on the hardened tarmac, over a portable pad that could take the high temperatures of takeoff. "We are scheduled for a 9:00 am arrival, so we need a takeoff around 8:53. You can always speed up, but you can't slow down," Steve quipped.

"We've got a pad there already, and we will drive the rest over now," Jesse waved to the big generator on the back of a semi trailer, "and meet you there around 10:00."

With little to do, Bess walked around the airport. Other pilots were making small talk around their planes in anticipation of doing flybys of the monument. She found her mind wandering, getting anxious about the flight, and thinking about all the events that had happened yesterday. She went back to her father and asked, "Can we take off a little early? Lets fly over to the beach and go up. We can fly over our house and the big dunes." Bess realized she hadn't seen much of the coast from the air yet.

The takeoff was easy, with the Starlighter rising fast into the late morning sun. Bess piloted it quickly over Roanoke Island. "Look down there," her father said, as he glanced out the windows. "That's the outdoor theater where they do that play, The Lost Colony." Bess saw an open amphitheater with wooden benches stretched across a semicircle facing a sandy stage. "We need to see that before we leave."

They crossed the sound with Bess navigating toward the big yellow sand dunes of Jockey's Ridge. "There's our beach house," Bess pointed out the big old cottage.

"Try not to go out too far over the ocean," her father insisted. "This thing doesn't float."

To the north, from their altitude, Bess could see the Wright Brothers Monument atop a green hill. It was distinctly different from the sandy hills that made up the rest of the barrier islands. "You take it," Bess told her father. "I know you want to fly over the monument." It was every pilot's dream, as well as an unspoken requirement to do a flyby of the monument, a tribute to the Wrights and their first flight of an airplane.

Steve took control of the Starlighter. It took two hands to fly the craft, which flew like both a helicopter and an airplane. He twisted the throttle handle to speed the craft up. The underside of the Starlighter began to thump rapidly where the chamber popped out sparks of superheated air, pushing the craft to several hundred miles an hour. Within moments, he was nearing the monument. "Let's give them a treat," he said.

In the seconds they had, Bess could see small groups of people standing on the side of the road by the monument, as well as a large number of them on the top on the hill. Steve turned the Starlighter to fly at an angle, exposing the big flashing chamber underneath to the spectators on the ground. Somewhere down there Lydia, Aurora, and Bess's mother watched as the Starlighter streaked by.

Steve slammed the Starlighter into a hard braking turn. He and Bess sunk into their seats before quickly turning back toward the monument. This time Steve took it slow. Everyone wanted to see the Starlighter in flight, and he was happy to show it off. He came back around, from the sound side this time. He approached over the old original takeoff spot that the Wrights had used in 1903. "See that big boulder?" Steve tilted the Starlighter to give Bess a better view. "That's where they took off from."

Bess saw a large white rock, near two small buildings out in the middle of a grassy field. "That's a hangar and shack that they just reconstructed. How'd you like to be out here in December, living in one of those?" Steve joked, but the commitment of the brothers in a harsh coastal winter couldn't be discounted.

"It would be neat to see, but I wouldn't want to stay there," Bess said. "I like our beach house just fine, thank you."

"Coming in for landing," Steve got them back on task. He circled the monument slowly. Bess could see a couple hundred people, most waving, but she was too far up to make out anyone individually.

The Starlighter settled in for a touchdown. He positioned the Starlighter over a big square of Marsden Mats, large metal rectangles used to create temporary roads or landing strips. A big bullseye painted in the middle marked their landing site. He pulled a lever to open the winglets, and cut the power. The Starlighter came floating down almost silently with the powerful engine turned off. It touched down like a feather, right in the middle of the landing pad.

Bess and Steve climbed out to wild cheering as people surrounded the Starlighter. To their back, a large number of spectators began to hurry down the paths of the hill to see them.

The morning went by quickly. First, Portia and the girls showed up after running down the hill. Then Jesse and the ground crew pulled in with the big semi truck and generator to provide extra power for the demonstrations they would do during the day.

After lunch, Bess looked around at the growing crowd. She had seen many of the same faces over and over. Now a few new people were showing up. She started recognizing new faces, tourists dressed in their idea of beach clothes, and locals in more casual t-shirts. Then she noticed one person who was somewhat in between. Not as fancy as a tourist, not as "local" as a local. He seemed very familiar, but also out of place. Bess couldn't figure out who he was or how she would know anyone around here when she had never been on the island before.

His face disappeared as someone walked in front of her.

"Hi!"

Bess recognized this face. It was Jamie from the marina, whom she had talked with about the strange shark attack. "Hi, Jamie!" Bess was happy to see the scientist. "Did you find out any more about that shark attack? Or the sea monster?"

Jamie laughed, "I'm sure there was nothing to that sea monster thing. And yes, I heard about your shark incident. That is a little distressing, especially this time of year. I'll be curious if it happens again.

"Now, can you tell me more about this incredible flying saucer?"

Bess started to correct her, "Starlight..." she never liked it when people called the Starlighter a flying saucer. But someone caught her eye. It wasn't the same man she saw before, but a younger, blond man, wearing tan linen shorts and a Hawaiian shirt, with gold and black sunglasses. He definitely looked like a tourist. Only Bess recognized him as someone else.

Then Bess looked for the other man she had seen before. He was walking up the big hill to the monument on top. She looked back at the blond, who smiled right at her, and nodded his head toward the path.

Bess made an excuse for leaving to Jamie and made her way up the hill.

"Hey, G-Man," Bess half whispered to the tall man she had followed up to the Wright Brothers Monument. She had figured out who the two men were. This one she had originally named The Chair, when she found him sitting in a chair in her father's study. Just at the base of the monument stood the younger blond, The Voice. Bess had heard him speaking first when the two men had met with her parents a few months ago. Their real names were Agents Marsh and Phillips. Bess casually called them 'the G-Men.' She knew they worked for the US government, maybe the FBI, but more likely something else.

Agent Marsh frowned at the term, but didn't correct her. "Are you having a good time?" he asked.

"Sure!" Bess answered. "Well..." she thought about the strange things that had happened since she got to the beach, and then asked him, "Why? Are you?" She nodded at the Hawaiian shirt clad partner. "I doubt The Voice down there is on vacation."

At that moment, four jets began screaming over the island from far to the north. Bess looked up to see the four pass in formation. She particularly noticed the shark shaped form of the body, accentuated with the painting of an open shark's mouth, similar to the old Flying Tigers of years ago.

When the noise cleared, Agent Marsh spoke up. "Yes, there may be people interested in what they can see around here." He nodded at the rapidly receding F-11s. "Including your *craft*." He specifically avoided using the term 'flying saucer.'

"And I understand you have had some rather interesting events here, too." He stared out at the blue ocean. It was a clear day, with blue skies meeting a dark blue sea. From atop Big Kill Devil Hill, the two could see far out to the horizon, over fifteen miles away. Just offshore, a few sailboats cruised with their white sails filled with wind. Farther out, sport fishing yachts sped through the waves, making white trails in the blue water. Farthest still, blurry in the far distant mist, hulking ships harvested seafood in large catches from the nets stretched into the deep Atlantic.

"Yes, well, I think that was just a weird coincidence," Bess shrugged. "Do you think something caused that shark stuff to happen?"

Agent Marsh said nothing, but pointed far out at the big ships on the horizon, more than twelve miles away.

"The fishermen?" Bess was incredulous, but she had learned to keep an open mind with what the G-Man would tell her. He knew a lot of things that most people didn't.

"Not fishermen," he said dully, but with a hidden gravity and importance. He handed Bess a pair of small binoculars to look out at the big fishing ships.

"Russians."

CHAPTER 8

Vacation Photos

Bess looked through the large binoculars at the big ships far out to sea. "Aren't they just those big fishing boats? I heard the fishermen say they were catching herring."

"They are," Agent Marsh agreed. "Those are certainly large scale commercial fishing ships out there, and they really are catching fish.

"But we also know that the Russians are always out with small trawlers, just into international waters, spying on us."

"Those don't look little," Bess commented.

"I agree," said Agent Marsh, "which is why I'm so suspicious.

"It's a long way to go to catch herring and mackerel, don't you think?"

Bess saw the grave look on Agent Marsh's face.

"And you want me to do something about it?" she asked. "You know I can't ride my horse out there," she hinted at an adventure she had several months earlier. "And I'm not flying the Starlighter out there. Like Dad said, that thing doesn't float."

"I know," Agent Marsh said soothingly, "I'm not going to ask you to do anything dangerous. I just want you to take a few pictures.

Bess jokingly responded, "Vacation snapshots?" as she held up an imaginary camera to her eye and took his picture.

"Something like that," Marsh laughed. "Just take the Starlighter up, get it level and still, and point and shoot," he made the gesture back at Bess, who smiled for the imaginary birdie.

Bess expected there to be a big group of people waiting to see her father and her take off, but the crowd was larger than she imagined. It actually helped her some as she watched so many people scurry around to find a spot that no one seemed to even notice Jesse carrying a medium sized metal box onto the Starlighter.

Bess and Steve climbed into the Starlighter to the cheers of the crowd. Steve smiled, happy with the attention, but only showing an Aw Shucks grin that went well with the Texas cowboy image he had. Aurora and Lydia screamed at Bess, wishing her a good flight, enjoying the attention their friend was getting. Bess looked around, trying to spot other

people in the crowd, but with the people so thick, and her father calling to her from inside, she gave up and climbed into her seat.

"Alright," said Steve positively, "Up and out. And get a few snapshots while we're at it." He nodded toward the strange oblong box of a camera attached to the instrument panel.

Steve again called to the local radio tower for permission to take off. There were lots of planes out during the day, and he didn't want to be in the path of a fast moving jet or a little prop plane, either. Bess heard the garbled squawk from the radio, which again included the strange side channel banter. It cleared, and the air controller announced that they were free to fly.

"Let's touch the sky." Bess punched the engine's ignition, and the Starlighter lifted off with a jolt, shooting high into the air. It cleared the height of the nearby monument in a second, and headed toward the clear blue above. Outside, Bess was sure that the crowd was making appreciative "ooohs" and "aaahs", but all she heard was the comforting heartbeat of the Starlighter below her.

"I've got the stick," Steve said, "You get to be Ansel Adams." He pointed at the strange camera on the panel. "Just press the lens up against the flat part of the glass, then put those ships out there on the two sights when they align. The camera will shoot real fast, and I'll hold the Starlighter still."

Bess lined up the cross hairs like the iron sights of a BB gun, and pressed the button. A motor whirred as inside the camera flipped through the shutter, spinning the film in the big can behind it. It took ten shots and was done.

"Dad, why do the G-men need us to take pictures?" Bess wondered. "Can't they just do this themselves?"

"Sure, but there are lots of reasons," Steve deftly began to manoeuvre the Starlighter, "Hang on, here comes the show," he paused in his explanation as the Starlighter revved up and took off to the north with a fast pulse of electrical pops from the discharge chamber beneath them. Bess sucked in her breath and hung on. Steve threw it into a wide turn to the west. It swung out over the sound, circling over the shallow waters. He flew a large circle, then settled the Starlighter into a slow flat flight.

"Wait," he looked at a local map, then the ground, "I want to show you something. Look down there, That's Kitty Hawk. See the church down there? So, that's where the Wright Brothers first came here from Ohio. They stayed in a house down there, and tested their first gliders on those sand dunes."

Bess looked down as Steve held the Starlighter at an angle, slowly orbiting the rolling dunes between a large forest and the wide sandy beach of the ocean side.

"Wow," breathed Bess. "It really must have been a different world back then." She hadn't had much time to learn about the Wrights when they were at Kitty Hawk. She only knew mostly from what she read, and what her father had talked about with her.

"You know, Orville Wright lived to see jets fly, and he even flew here once for the anniversary of flight on a plane that had a bigger wingspan than his first flight. He really got to see the fruits of their work. It's a reason we celebrate his birthday today. He was a really well respected man. He did a lot of work with NACA, too.

"Of course, Wilbur was the better pilot. He probably would tell us to stop talking and fly faster."

"Then you better let me take over," teased Bess. She grabbed the controls, feeling them come alive in her hands as her father let go. She twisted the throttle and said, "Up and out!"

The Starlighter lifted higher, then dipped, adding speed. Bess zoomed the craft back toward Big Kill Devil Hill and the monument on top, bringing it up to top speed. The crowd wanted a treat, and she was going to deliver.

At 500 miles per hour, the Starlighter was a shiny blur with a blinding pinprick of light at the bottom, blinking like a purple strobe. Bess flew past the monument and threw the ship into a hard braking move, lifting the leading edge, making the air compress and smoke around the outer ring. It left a short tunnel of water vapor in its wake. The Starlighter dipped and floated like a feather in the wind back to the monument. She flew over the hill, then to the boulder that marked the takeoff spot of the Wright Flyer, where the first flights took place. She saw a few people around the boulder taking pictures of her, so she waved out the window and smiled broadly.

"I gotcha," Steve took control of the Starlighter so Bess could look around. He slowly let it rise up so Bess could see the entirety of the historic site. The big rock marked the takeoff, with three markers showing the first three flights, and far off in the distance, a fourth, the last flight, by Wilbur. "He was the better pilot," Bess agreed.

"Hey, when we land, I want to walk over here and get some pictures of the shacks and the marker, okay Dad?"

"Sure thing, kiddo. Let's go put her down and get recharged. We have to fly back to Manteo before dark."

Bess leaned over the window and took a picture with her little Kodak. "Just like what the Wright Brothers saw."

Steve landed the Starlighter in the calm nook of the hill. It touched down as usual, soft and quiet as a feather. He still remembered his first landing of the Starlighter. It had been quiet, but not as soft. "It's a lot nicer at the beach," he thought. "Soft sand, no cactus."

Bess hopped out to cheers and waves. Her friends quickly found her and gathered her out of the crowd. "How was it?" asked Jesse.

"Great! We saw where the Wright Brothers first stayed over in Kitty Hawk, and I even hovered over their take off spot. I got some great pictures."

Bess saw Jamie the ichthyologist walk by and wave. Jamie was glancing around at the Starlighter, making a face that she was impressed by the flight.

"Hey, let's go over to see the first flight spot on the other side of the hill," Aurora insisted. The others agreed. Lydia pulled Bess by the wrist, her little Kodak dangling by a strap.

The four of them had fun looking in the little shack that the Wrights used when they were testing their gliders and plane. Jesse stood in the hangar next door, his arms outstretched to show how big it was. "I don't know how they fit the plane in here!"

"I think they put it in sideways," said Bess, as she took his picture.

"Okay, watch this," Aurora exclaimed. "I'm gonna run from here to the first spot. See if I can go faster that Orville Wright. It took him twelve seconds."

Jesse looked at his watch, and then said, "Go!" with a wave of his hand. Aurora, a natural athlete, was much faster. All four took their turns beating Orville's time, but no one was faster than Aurora.

"You didn't have a six hundred pound plane and a headwind," explained Bess. "I bet he was going 30 miles per hour." Always the pilot, Bess understood the difference between running on the ground and flying into the air.

The four asked a tourist to take their picture by the big boulder that sat on the take off site. "I wonder how they got the plane around this rock?" asked Lydia, jokingly, but with a dead serious face.

Jesse looked at her incredulously at first, then realized she was trying to get them to respond. "They probably just lifted it," he said back. "They seem like real strong dudes."

Back at the Starlighter, Bess sat her camera down on a table near their big generator truck. The big engine hummed with power as it fed the batteries to the aircraft. She looked up to see her father coming over. "Do you want to fly back with me? Or stay here and go to the beach with the rest of the Zap-Gun Rangers?" Steve made a big circle with his hand, taking in the four kids.

"I'll..." Bess looked over her dad's shoulder. "Hey, someone's in the Starlighter."

All of them took off running. Steve reached the ship first, followed by Aurora and the rest of the group. He jumped up and in the ship, grabbing at the mysterious figure in the cockpit.

"Hey!" It was a kid's scream. A young boy had climbed up and was trying to sit in the pilot's seat.

"Hold on there, little partner," Steve tried to calm the boy who had been caught and was now nervous and near tears. He looked like he was only 7 or

8. "This is no place for you." Steve gently but with the firmness of a cowboy on a calf guided the shaken little kid out of the Starlighter. "Where's your mama?" he asked softly.

"I wasn't going to do anything!" The boy cried. "A lady told me I could. She said I could sit in it. It can't take off with the wires on it." He pointed to the big power cables.

Bess and the rest of the kids walked back over to the power truck with the scared boy. She looked around the table, and noticed something. "Hey, my camera is gone."

"What lady told you to get in there? Your mama?" Steve asked again. The little boy started crying, sniffling his nose and wiping it on a dirty sleeve.

"Hold on," Lydia pushed the others out of the way. "It's alright. You're not in trouble, bud. Don't worry." Lydia, with her soft blonde hair flowing in the wind and bright smile, calmed the little kid some. Just then, his mother ran up.

"Oh, I'm so sorry!" she cried. "He got away from me in this crowd. I was so worried he climbed the hill. I don't know if I could make it all the way up there to look for him. He didn't break anything, did he?"

"No, it's fine," Steve said. "Did you tell him he could go in the cockpit?"

"No!" the boy answered. "It wasn't her." He seemed worried he would get his mom into more trouble. "It was another lady. It was her!"

He pointed out to the road. Everyone followed his finger, but all they saw was a door closing on an old black car. It quickly sped off toward the beach.

CHAPTER 9

Ghost Lights

Everyone was sad and upset when Bess had her camera stolen. "Who would want my little Kodak? It's not like you can't get them anywhere!" She was mostly upset that she lost all her photos of her friends at the monument. "We'll have to come back and take more later," suggested Aurora.

Bess decided to ride to the beach house with her friends instead of flying back with her father. She had enough excitement for one day.

Back at the beach house, they gathered for late lunch. Portia made the kids a stack of baloney and cheese sandwiches. She was out of her element with the seafood that the locals seemed to consume regularly, but was happy to make something simple for the four teens.

"Hey, thanks, Mrs. Truly, they're great," complimented Jesse.

"Yes, truly nifty," joked Aurora.

"Thanks, Mom!" Bess kissed her mother on the cheek.

"Thank you, Mrs. Truly," said Lydia, "I'll get us some sodas."

"It's quite alright," Portia said softly. Bess's mother was smart, and clever, and often appeared stern as she thought through things, but around her daughter and friends she was incredibly kind. She knew at their age, they needed both some satisfaction from adventure, and trust from adults to make their own decisions, as long as they knew what they were doing. She had brought Bess up to trust her own decisions once she had analyzed the problem, then act accordingly. Bess had never disappointed her. And Portia knew Bess and her friends would always look out for each other.

"I'm sorry about your camera, dear. You can use mine until we get you a new one."

Bess smiled, but felt guilty. "I don't want to take it from you, Mom."

"You should have one to capture the moments with your friends, and I want you to know that it wasn't your fault that it was taken." Portia was kind with her words, but insistent. "It's got film in it, but I haven't used it yet. You'd be doing me a favor if you took some vacation photos."

"I still wonder who would take it? Like, who would want your photos?" Jesse pondered the question.

"Do you think that boy had anything to do with it? Like a distraction?" asked Aurora.

Lydia shook her head, blonde curls fluttering in a frizzy cloud from the humid beach. "That little curtain climber was scared out of his mind. I don't know who put him up to that, but he wasn't trying to steal anything."

"Yeah, I'm betting it was some wet rag who wanted it," suggested Jesse, with a tone of finality. "Look, let's get that out of our minds. Let's go for a swim."

After lunch, the four changed into their swimsuits and went to the beach. Even though it was later in the afternoon, the sun still hung high in the summer sky, and heat permeated the air. The sand felt burning hot along the dunes. Even with their tennis shoes on, the sand scattered into their shoes and on their ankles. They ended up running to the firm sand that was cooler with the ocean waves that lapped to the shore. Aurora threw her towel down on the sand, then cried out, "Hey, lookit that!"

She pointed at a large hole in the sand, covered with tiny scratches around the hole.

"What?" asked Lydia. She looked at the hole. "It's just a... AAAHHH!"

Lydia screamed out a startled shriek as a big strange crab crawled out and kicked a bit of sand out of the hole. It was yellow and white, colored almost exactly like the sand, with white pincers almost as bright as teeth. On the front of the shell were two black eyes that looked like tiny beads. Startled, it ducked back into the hole.

"What was that?!" Lydia looked down at her feet, now terrified at what might be under her.

"He's cool," said Aurora, "Come back out, little Crabby-O." She tried calling to the strange crab, but it wouldn't show itself.

"I'm getting in the water," decided Lydia. "There may be crabs there, too, but at least I can keep my feet up."

They all agreed, and jumped into the calm ocean waves. The afternoon must have soothed the shore break, for the waves were only tiny rivulets, not even a foot high. The water was incredibly warm from the hot sun shining on the ocean all day. "I'm going to float until the moon comes out," declared Lydia. "And then, I'm staying in a bit longer. At least until those crabs go away."

"You gotta remember," Bess said, "It's their home. We're just visiting."

"I know," Lydia agreed. "It's just... they're creepy looking."

They were in and out of the water for about an hour, when Bess spied two horses and riders coming from the north down the beach. She almost immediately recognized her new friend Vicki. The riders trotted up to the four of them. "Hey, Vicki!"

"Hi, Bess!" Vicki waved at the others, and Bess introduced them. "This is my little sister, Sasha."

A thin girl of about thirteen smiled shyly and said "hi" with a soft wave. She looked like a dusty thin twin of her older sister. They both wore jeans and t shirts, but were barefoot in the stirrups of their horses.

Bess said to Sasha, "You have a nice horse." She admired the chestnut mare. "What's her name?"

Sasha immediately brightened now that she had something to talk about. "This is Elly. She's named after Elynor Dare."

Sasha said the name like everyone knew who that was. Vicki said, "She was one of the original colonists. You need to go see The Lost Colony."

Sasha, now comfortable around the strangers, said, "I was in it last year!"

"Vicki," Lydia changed the subject, "what are those crabs that are crawling around the beach? They sure are strange looking."

"Aw, those are ghost crabs!" she laughed.

Lydia made a face. "They're ghosts! There really are ghosts everywhere on this island!"

"No," Vicki laughed, "they're ghost *crabs*. They won't hurt you, less you try to grab one. They come out at night. They're just part of the beach.

"Tell ya what, I need to take Sasha home..."

"You don't need to *take* me," Sasha complained. "I know how to get home."

"I have to take you home. And I need to go home. Can I come over later tonight? I can show you why they are ghost crabs. You'll need some flashlights."

Bess and her friends smiled at each other. "I think we can find something."

The sun had just set behind the distant sand dunes when Vicki's father dropped her off at Bess's beach house. After meeting Bess's parents and making sure she could get a ride home, Vicki said goodbye to her father, and pulled out a flashlight. "Okay, this is fun. Let's go explore the beach. It's different at night. You got flashlights?"

Jesse picked up a dented chrome flashlight off the fireplace mantle. "I've got mine," he said.

"What about you three?" Vicki asked.

Bess, Lydia, and Aurora all walked to the hallway and pulled down three belts with holsters. Inside were their Zap-Guns, an invention of Bess's mother.

"We got that covered," Bess said. Vicki stared wide eyed at the strange devices. "Come out here on the porch. I'll show you."

Stepping outside, Bess turned the dial on her Zap-Gun to the lowest setting, then she pointed it out into the dark and squeezed the trigger. The emitter barrel lit up with a bright purple glow, illuminating the sandy back of the house all the way to the dune.

"My mom invented these. Technically, it's static discharge device, but my Dad nicknamed them Zap-Guns, like the outer space ray guns. We use them on the ranch. They're good for fixing fences, digging a post hole, and lighting up the night, like this." Bess left out some of the more dangerous times she had to use the tool.

"Wild!" Vicki cooed at the sight. "Those ghost crabs aren't gonna know what hit them! Come on, this'll be fun."

The five kids ran out onto the now dark beach. The sand had cooled to where the kids felt their toes grow cold. Only Vicki, the local beach girl, seemed used to it. The moon was not yet up, so the stars twinkled brightly in the dark sky. To the north and south, fishing piers sent out bright lights into the water for the evening fishermen and women to cast lines out to the late night denizens of the Outer Banks Atlantic.

"Now, watch," Vicki commanded. She switched on her light and shone it into the beach sand. In her beam, she caught first one, then two, them more, of the strange white and yellow creatures out in the sand. Lydia gave a muffled shriek, and grabbed Aurora's arm. "They all come out at night,"Vicki explained. "There's fewer predators and threats. They're scavengers. They eat the fish that wash up, or junk the tourists leave."

"So... they are kind of like vultures?" Aurora half asked, half commented.

"I guess so," answered Vicki. "Here, see that one? You all shine your lights on it. Circle it."

Bess turned on her Zap-Gun, as did the other girls. Jesse turned on his flashlight. When the five formed a ring around the poor ghost crab, it froze in the dazzling lights. "Okay, now shoo it over to me."

Lydia was adamant, "But... it might pinch you!"

"Don't worry, why would it pinch me unless I pick it up?"

Jesse stomped his foot, and the big crab scurried over toward Vicki, who had turned her light off. The others followed it with their lights as it ran straight across her bare feet. "See?" she wiggled her toes. "Still got all ten!"

The group had fun chasing down the nighttime creatures. Vicki explained that they really were crabs, and had gills, but got their oxygen from the moisture in the sand, and that they would drown in the ocean. "So don't let them go into the waves."

After that, Lydia changed from fearing them to continually trying to scoot them away from the surf. "Run, little babies, run!" she commanded.

After about an hour, Bess and the rest of the gang were tired and sandy. They stood in the wet shallow wash. "The water is warmer than the sand," Aurora noticed.

"Water holds heat longer," Lydia commented.

"Whoa, what's that?" Bess said, pointing to the horizon.

"Oh my gosh, it's a ghost ship!" Lydia exclaimed.

"No, don't worry, it's just the moon coming up," explained Vicki. "Sometimes we get lucky and see a full moon come boiling out of the ocean."

The five watched as the moon slowly arose in a wavy orange haze. The ocean was smooth as glass, and reflected the light with barely a ripple. All of them were silent as they watched it rise up and change color.

"It's so... big..." Jesse commented.

As they watched the moon rise, the kids suddenly saw a shape roll into view near the shore. A large silhouette crossed in front of the moon, a big, black, and broken mass rolled toward the beach.

CHAPTER 10

Shadow Of A Sea Monster

The big shape rolled and tumbled just off shore. A large and unstable black beast, staggering as if in a fight with the current that ran sluggishly across the beach, determined to push the strange monster to shore.

"What is that?" Lydia called out. She had already been frightened by sharks and crabs. A giant hulking sea monster was too much for her. A sudden terrible wail from the shape only made her worse.

"Oooouuuuuuhh..." was all they heard.

The shape passed in front of the rising moon. It was huge, with a large pointed nose, and a tall jagged middle, but the back end looked torn and broken. Thin posts, like whiskers of an enormous catfish, stuck out, broken, at all angles.

Bess ran toward it, seeing the silhouette in the moonlight. "It's a boat!" She cried. "It's been in a shipwreck!"

The broken fishing boat foundered in the closing shallow surf. The water was only a few feet deep, and it seemed to reach up and grab the keel of the big yacht. It wobbled and splashed as the ocean tried to push it free. She snapped her Zap-Gun up one setting, and squeezed the trigger. A bright light came out, a mix of bright blue and white, illuminating the entire boat.

What they saw was carnage. The boat was broken in many places. It was amazing the craft was still in one piece. The entire transom was ripped off in a big half circle. The tower on top of the hard top was twisted beyond recognition, just a mass of pipes and lines. The captain's helm was opened, with the hard top ripped and gone. The bow, long and sleek to cut through the Atlantic's waves, was cracked, gashed, and broken open.

The five kids stared, dumbfounded, unable to do anything with the boat just offshore. Then, in the harsh light of Bess's Zap-Gun, a hand came up above the gunwale of the boat. Lydia let out a cut off shriek, startled by the horrific sight of just an arm, dirty and wet, appearing in the light.

"Oh no," Bess cried, "someone's on board that boat."

After a moment of stunned silence, the four kids found themselves in their element. They organized quickly. Bess commanded them, "Aurora, Lydia, run up to the house, get lights, see if we have a long rope in the garage, and call the police..."

"I can do better," Vicki said, "the station is just on the other side of the road. I'll go and show them where we are." Without waiting for agreement, Vicki took off at a run.

Bess let her go, wishing they had one horse to speed things up. "Jesse," she looked at her friend with a stern glare of fear and concern, "we have to get to that boat. Do you think we can swim out there?"

"I can, but you need to stay here," he said. "I need light to see where I'm going. That boat isn't far off from shore. I may be able to wade out there." He already began pulling his shirt over his head.

Jesse was well into the water, while Bess shown her light out into the ocean. The spooky hand had disappeared. Bess worried the person may be seriously injured. It felt like forever for Bess to stand, helpless on the beach, while the boat drifted and churned in the shallow ocean wash.

It was a strange moment of emptiness and silence. Jesse was out in the water, barely visible in the inky black ocean against the stark white boat. Behind her, Lydia and Aurora had run to the beach house, and Vicki, the only person who really knew their way around, had run off to find the local police station. At Bess's feet stood a ghost crab, large and white, its beady black eyes looking warily at Bess, frozen and unsure to run or stay.

Then, in a fit of panic, it took off toward the dry sand. Bess let it run close to her, not willing to move her feet away from the white pinching claws. It scurried to a hole, completely unconcerned with Bess.

She realized a moment later why it ran. Behind her, footsteps thudded the soft sand. She looked over her shoulder, keeping the light of the Zap-Gun fixed on the ship, and saw several figures running toward her. Aurora caught up with and passed her father, who was carrying an immense length of rope tied into an itchy figure eight. Behind him came Lydia, and farther back, her mother strode with authority while trying to keep her balance in the soft sand.

Bess looked out at the boat as soon as Aurora and her father got to her. Jesse had reached the boat, and it rolled and moved strangely. Steve called out, "Watch it, Jesse! Don't let that thing get on top of you! Go around to the stern! The back!"

Jesse seemed to hear, and he moved away from the dancing bow. If the boat found its way off the sandbar, it could easily roll over on Jesse, pinning him under the water. It was a dangerous situation. Jesse was brave, but out of his element in the rolling salt water waves.

It was a fortunate act on his part. The boat was freed from the sandbar, and began to roll, moving out and toward the south. Jesse reached up to grab a part of the hull. He pulled himself up, then fell back. From the beach, everyone could see him grasp his arm.

He looked at it and then, seemingly unfazed, used his other arm to grab something on what was left of the transom, to pull him up and over the boat. He disappeared for a moment as he knelt down behind the gunwale. Coming back up, he waved, first signaling he found the man on board, then yelling, "He's alive!"

Even from the distance, everyone understood Jesse. He put his leg up and pointed to it. Portia arrived and immediately deciphered the meaning. "Is there a sailor on that ship? He must have an injured leg."

"How are we going to get him in?" asked Lydia. "That boat is too far out to swim him to shore."

Bess noticed another, even more pressing problem

"It's drifting back out to sea.

"And Jesse is going to be stuck on it!"

CHAPTER 11

A Broken Chandelier

"We have to get that rope to him," said Steve. The boat seemed to be moving more quickly to the south now.

"There's no way we can swim out there, not that fast," said Aurora, who was already thinking of diving in to chase the boat down. She knew it would be futile, but she wasn't going to let her friend just drift away into the dark night.

"No, no one is going out there," Steve insisted. His daughter and her friends did a lot of daring things, but it was always around their home town, not in the ocean thousands of miles away. He wasn't going to let them take that much of risk of swimming into the darkness.

"How far out is that boat?" Bess asked.

"About 100 feet," Steve estimated.

"And how long is that rope?" she nodded at the big coil of sailing line his father had.

"Probably 200 feet," he hefted the rope.

"Alright, I got an idea," Bess said. She looked at her mom, who stood, expressionless. Portia would always stand back and let Bess figure out problems, because Bess was good at that. Only if she knew something would either work better, or wouldn't work, would Portia offer her advice. She knew to trust Bess to do the right thing.

"Tie the end into a knot, a big one, big as you can, tight, too."

Her father said, "There's no way we can throw it that far, kiddo."

"I'm not going to throw it."

She waved for Aurora to come next to her. "Take this," she handed the big knotted end of the rope, a round lump bigger than her fist, to her friend. "Lydia, you keep the light on the boat."

Lydia dialed her Zap-Gun up one notch and shone it out to Jesse and the boat.

"C'mon," she ran out into the shallow surf. "I want you to throw that rope out as far as you can, a big arc."

"I don't think I can get it to the boat," Aurora said, staring at Jesse as he kept drifting away.

"You won't have to, just a good hard toss over the water."

Aurora braced herself, then began to spin the heavy weighted rope. She had to be careful not to hit in in the water or wet sand and have it lose its momentum. Bess stood back just a few feet to give her room.

Aurora felt the weight, knew that it was spinning as fast as it could without her losing control, and then she tossed it. The rope sped out over the black ocean in a perfect low arc. Tiny bits of sea spray shot off as the rope pulled taught. It made a soft whipping sound as the spread out other end spooled itself over the water.

As strong and accurate a throw as it was, there was no way the rope would travel that far. No one could throw it a hundred feet. They all watched, all with frowns of dejection on their faces.

Except for Portia, who smiled secretly and slyly at her daughter. And Bess, who wore a grim look of determination.

Bess whipped her Zap-Gun out and spun the dial midway up the power settings, squeezing the focusing lens at the end. With quick aim, she fired right next to the flying rope. The blue lightning flew out of the barrel, following a straight path to the big knotted end of the rope. With a pop, it hit the weighted end, shooting it far out to the ocean. The long tail of the rope lit up with the static electricity.

If Bess and her friends had ever heard of St. Elmo's Fire, the static charge of sails on old ships from lightning strikes that made the masts glow, they would have known what they were seeing.

What they did see was the rope fly like a little comet right up and over the aft deck of the boat. It landed on top of Jesse's shoulder, and he gathered the rope up in his hands and searched for a place to tie it off.

"Use the cleat," Steve shouted. "A figure eight around the cleat! It'll lock itself off!"

Jesse twisted the rope around the metal cleat at what was left of the aft of the boat, hoping it didn't tear the rest of the transom off.

"Okay, let's pull!" Bess shouted.

"No, wait," Steve said, "Pull it taut, but no more. Get on this side," he pointed to the north side of the rope, as the boat pulled the line to the south. "Don't get caught with that rope around you!"

In the distance, they saw a flashing light and headlights bouncing down the beach. Vicki had found the police.

"Dig a hole, quick," Steve said. Everyone but Lydia, who kept her Zap-Gun steady on the boat and Jesse, began to dig a deep hole. Just below the soft sand, the pebbles became wet and course, jamming under fingernails and scratching knuckles, but no one slowed. Once they had a three foot hole, Steve tossed an anchor in from the other end of the rope. The strange anchor had two pointed blades that flopped into the sand, attached to a bar in the middle, and the rope came up from that. "Now, fill it in. Pack it tight. That anchor will bite into the sand and hopefully hold the boat until we can get something bigger to pull it in."

With the anchor buried, the group watched as the rope slowly pulled out. Then it went tight, and the rope moved. It scratched across the sand, smoothing out all the footprints as it pulled hard to the south.

Bess watched carefully to see if the anchor would come up, but the sand stayed firm and packed down. The boat even began to be pulled toward shore until it wedged again on a sandbar in the shallows.

It would take time to get a truck with a winch to pull the broken fishing yacht to shore. The poor sailor was in bad shape, with a broken leg, a bump on his head, lots of cuts, and dehydration. The police officer and a sheriff's deputy loaded him into a truck and carefully drove him to the road where he could be transported to a hospital. He was badly hurt, and couldn't speak about what had happened.

The wrecked boat was pulled up onto the dry beach and secured with ropes and anchors, so it wouldn't float away and hit a pier or endanger anything in the night. The group of adults and teens examined the wreck under the bright light of the girls' Zap-Guns and the now risen moon.

"The whole transom is torn off," Steve said. "I'm amazed it still floated."

The entire back of the fishing boat, where fish would have been stored after they were caught, was gone. It was torn in ragged bits, in a semicircle.

"Look at the shape," Aurora said, "It almost looks like it was bitten off. You don't think..." she trailed off her words, afraid to say the rest.

"No, it's unlikely that shark did this," Portia answered the unspoken question. "This is far too much damage. It's almost like an impact, but not quite." Portia, always a scientist, would wait until she had enough information before making a guess as to the cause.

"Phew," Lydia said, "I've had enough sharks, thank you."

"Look at this," Bess shone her Zap-Gun into the remains of the well for holding fish and bait. A few dead dolphin were all that remained inside. She pointed at the area around the fish. "See how it sparkles?"

"Isn't that just ice?" asked Jesse, still dripping and sandy from his ordeal. He held a bandage on his arm where he scraped it climbing in the boat. "They pack the fish on ice when they catch them."

"All the ice would have melted by now. Or escaped out the back." Bess said. She reached down to pick one up.

It was firm, pointed, and clear as she shone her light through it. It felt a little like plastic, but heavier, too. "It's like a crystal, but without that brittleness," she said.

Portia looked closely. The rest of the group crowded around, looking over her shoulder as she shone a light deep into it. It gave off a soft blue hue. Even with all the damage to the boat, it was unscratched. It was shaped like a triangle, with a strange curved base, almost as if it had been attached to something else. "It looks... man-made," she said offhand. "See the slight waves in there? But it's not a plastic or created crystal. It almost looks like," she shone a tightened beam through the crystal, onto the white boat. "It almost looks like aluminum, but it can't be that..."

She thought, wondering, and the rest were silent. It wasn't like Portia to take this much time to come to an answer. "I'd like to get this under a spectrometer, but it almost looks like sapphire."

"You know what it looks like to me," Jesse said casually as he stared under his bandage.

He reached over Bess's shoulder to the big clear triangle. His finger traced around the bottom, touching the two sides, one then the other, going up to the strange curved point on top.

"It looks like a giant shark's tooth."

CHAPTER 12

Sea Hunt

Tired and sore from her ghost crab hunt that turned into an ocean rescue, Bess went to bed and fell into a deep sleep, dreaming of crabs turning into tiny crystalline sharks on the beach as she tiptoed her way to a shore made of glass. She was relieved to wake up early the next morning.

Her father was taking her out to go fishing on the charter he arranged. Steve seemed undaunted by the events of the night before. Shipwrecks and strange events seemed only to intrigue him. Being from Texas originally, then a fighter pilot in World War II, and finally living in the dry prairie of New Mexico, a churning ocean filled with bobbing ships, strange sea creatures, and a sense of adventure only fueled the man.

"No way you'd get me out there," exclaimed Lydia when she was asked if she wanted to go.

"I'll go," Jesse complained, "but I don't think I should go catch fish with this cut on my arm." His wound was superficial, but the long gash was sore and needed time to heal.

"Well, I'm still up for it," said Aurora encouragingly. "I'll probably never get a chance to do this again, so I'm game."

An hour later Bess, Aurora, and Steve were on board the fishing boat, churning out of Oregon Inlet. Bess saw an early ferry running tourists and locals over to the next island. The passengers spilled from their cars for the short trip and stood along the sides of the ferry, waving at the fast fishing boat as it passed by to the stern. Bess waved back. She wondered what adventures they were on. How simple or complex would their day be? Did they even know about the strange shipwreck of the night before?

"Did they find the other people from that boat?? Bess asked the captain as he finally cleared the rough waters of the inlet and powered his way into the warm Gulf Stream and its promise of schools of fish ready to be hooked and reeled in.

"Yeah," said Captain Tillett, "They found'em in a life raft 'baout as soon as sun come up." His brogue came out thick on his ship. He was content in his element with the salt spray hitting him in his sunglasses. "They said they all tried to get into the life raft, but got pushed away, and that poor mate of his couldn't get on 'cause of his broke leg."

"Did they ever find out what happened to them?" asked Steve.

Captain Tillett scratched under his cap, an obvious sign of disbelief. His mate, a teenage boy, snorted a course laugh of contempt. Finally, Captain Tillett said, "Yeah..." he stretched it out, almost hoping that he wouldn't have to say it. "Them fellahs said the water just came alive, jumped onto the boat, and bit the transom off."

"Whoa..." breathed Aurora.

"That's, that's impossible," said Bess. Then she internally took back the statement. She had seen enough to know that it very well could be possible.

"Oi said that, too," said Captain Tillett. "Sea monsters, giant jellyfish, transparent whales, whatever they're sayin', something happened out there, and they don't want anyone to know what really happened."

The boat plowed on into relative silence among the charter and crew. The steady rumble of the diesel and the rushing wash of waves across the long bow was almost calming enough to take the events of the past day off their minds.

The morning passed quickly. Captain Tillett got them to the fishing grounds in record time. He and the mate organized the poles and got the lines out. Steve was looking for eating fish. Other people went out to get billfish, marlin, sailfish, or swordfish, but he wanted to catch something to cook and eat.

"We gotcha, rigged for dolphin," the mate said confidently.

"I'm still not used to that," said Aurora. "I need to remember that it's dolphin *fish*, not dolphin *mammal*."

"Oi can call it a dorado, if yeh loike," joked the mate. "Some of the old toimers call it that."

"Oh, no, I'll get it," insisted Aurora. "Whatever the locals say is right with me."

It was a good thing that Aurora got used to calling them dolphin, because Captain Tillett really put them on the fish. Within an hour they had found a school and started pulling in the fish. Bess and Aurora got good at reeling in lines when Steve had hooked a large fish, and they all ended up catching several of the yellow and green dolphin.

"We're gonna eat tonight!" Steve exclaimed when he reeled in a particularly large male, with deep green and yellow marking and a big blunt head.

After lunch, Bess and Aurora gave in to a sunny day and sat out on the long bow of the boat, sunning themselves in the heat of the day. Steve had Captain Tillett chasing after some other fish, hoping to find a tuna somewhere. Bess looked out over the bow at other ships and boats farther out to sea.

"What are they fishing for?" she asked.

"The other boats like us are charters, probably catching the same thing. They could be after billfish, too." Captain Tillett pointed to the north, far out into the deep ocean. "Those are big fishery ships, international ones, could be herring, pogies, maybe tuna."

Bess made a mental note of the ships. They were the same ones she had photographed the day before.

"Wow, what's that?!" Aurora pointed out to sea. A long black line skimmed along the surface of the water. It looked like a shadow of something large just under the water, moving at incredible speed. "That's not the sea monster, is it?"

Everyone stopped to look out to where Aurora pointed. The black shape flew across the water at high speed, much faster than any boat. It had a dark form like a head, and the rest of the shape flowed out from behind, like a gauzy cape.

"Aw, them is just sea ducks," said the mate. "They can go 50, maybe 70 miles an hour."

Bess watched in admiration at how the flock stayed together at only inches above the water.

Then, with a sudden splash, the flock scattered. Like shadowy black confetti, a huge wave had knocked them up into the sky!

CHAPTER 13

The Invisible Predator

Everyone on the boat saw the giant splash. Aurora still had to ask, "Did you see that?!" It looked like the ocean just exploded upward, sending all the little black sea ducks scattering into the sky.

"What was that, an explosion?" Jesse cried out.

"No explosion, we would have heard something, or felt it," said Bess. Captain Tillett nodded in agreement.

All of them scanned the water for a cause. Bess, with her sharp eyes, saw it a moment before Aurora. She pointed, "Look, over there."

She could see a slim shape in the water, creating a high speed wake. It moved like the sea ducks, only this time she was sure it was under the water. A small ridge raised up, a bow wake of something incredibly fast moving just below the surface.

"It looks like a torpedo," Captain Tillett said in amazement. "But if it exploded, it wouldn't still be moving."

"Do you think it's a whale? Or a shark?" Aurora asked.

"No whale can move that fast. And there are only a couple sharks that big, and they move slow, too."

It quickly sunk in to all of them that the stories of sailors spotting a sea monster may be all too real.

"Do you want to go see what it was?" asked Aurora. Her curiosity often got her into chasing things that she shouldn't always chase.

"Uh... no... I think we might want to head back to the marina. Do you mind calling your fishing trip short?" Captain Tillett asked. "I can give you some of your money back."

"No need," Steve said. He had caught most of what he wanted. "You use the same amount of fuel either way. I'm not taking food out of your mouth, skipper." Steve didn't add that he, too, felt more comfortable heading toward land.

The trip back in was somber and quiet, as quiet as the trip out, but for more personal reasons. Contemplating how some other sailors claimed to have been attacked by a strange sea monster was one thing. Seeing something out in the ocean, something they couldn't understand, that was different. It became personal to the group.

Bess and Aurora stared out from the stern. They were wondering and curious if the strange shape they saw would still be out there, instead of disappearing to the north.

The young mate kept his weather eye out as well, while he secured the poles and cleaned the deck. He kept his words to himself for a moment, but his body language spoke volumes. He wasn't so much wondering if the sea monster was out there, more so concerned that the thing they saw might follow them, and find them. While Bess hoped to get a glance at the creature, the mate hoped he wouldn't.

"Yeh know," he finally spoke, making Bess and Aurora jump, he had been so quiet, "this reminds me of an old legend. You hear of the Flaming Ship of Ocracoke?"

Bess shook her head no, and Aurora brightened from a tempered frown to a bright smile. Anything for a distraction, she thought.

"A long toime ago," he began, with his wonderful Outer Banks brogue softening the "i"s into "oi"s, "there was this ship that was taking people from Europe, refugees from a war, over to New Bern." He pointed vaguely south, referring to a town somewhere along the coast, Bess guessed. "The captain and crew killed them all and robbed them, then set foire to the ship to hide their crime.

"When they all got into the loifeboats, the ship started to sail towards them. It ran into the boats, spillin' all the pirates into the ocean. Only two of them made it to shore near Ocracoke down there," again he pointed, "and they confessed right before they died roight on the shore.

"Naow, every full moon in September, the ship reappears, all on foire, but never burned. It sails in toward Ocracoke, then turns north, just like that thing did. It disappears into the noight, like a ghost or wraith. They say it's the refugees, still a'tryin' to get to land and the home they wanted."

Aurora stood with her mouth agape. "Wow," she said breathlessly.

"Have you ever seen it?" Bess asked. She didn't necessarily believe in the ghost stories she heard, but the Outer Banks was a strange and mysterious land. She couldn't discount any legend.

"One toime," the mate went on, with a mischievous smile he couldn't quite hide, "I was out on the beach, and saw something roise up out of the horizon. It was a big orange glow that disappeared into a low cloud. Oi'm not sayin' it was, but Oi'm not sayin' it wasn't." With that mysterious non answer, he left to go to the bridge with Captain Tillett.

Bess and Aurora looked at each other and giggled. It was the best way to ease the tension as they hit the first waves going into Oregon Inlet.

Steve Truly left Captain Tillett and his mate with a large tip for a very interesting day. They also left with a cooler packed tightly with ice and enough dolphin fillets to eat for a month. "We'll get these packed into the freezer at the house, and pull out some to cook tonight," Steve said as they drove back to the beach house.

The afternoon passed quickly into early evening. Everyone could tell that Steve was anxious to get a fire going on the new Weber grill out on the back porch. The big black dome grill had only been around a few years, but Steve had embraced the outdoor cooker like so many others had. A gleam came across his face as he lit the charcoal in the bottom of the round grill.

While he prepared the food and cooking utensils, Bess, Aurora, and Jesse filled in the events of the day to Portia and Lydia.

"See? I'm glad I didn't go," exclaimed Lydia. But then she admitted, "But I would like to see what has been causing all these problems."

"We may get an answer," said Portia cryptically.

The kids looked at her. Portia's face said nothing, until she nodded slightly toward the front of the house. Down the driveway came a long black sedan. It seemed quite out of place compared to the flashy station wagons of tourists and worn trucks of the locals. "Who is that?" Jesse wondered out loud.

"I'll give you two guesses," hinted Portia.

Bess thought for a moment, then laughed at the clue. When the car stopped, two men, now easily recognizable in their black suits, got out. Agents Marsh and Phillips were on the case, it seemed.

Steve was undaunted by the addition of two more guests. He already had more grilled dolphin than he thought he would need, but was having so much fun cooking that he kept throwing more fillets on the grill. They came off light and flaky, with perfect little crisscrosses of grill marks, and hints of salt and a tangy red seasoning that was popular on the east coast. He prepared a stack of fish sandwiches slathered in tartar sauce, along with a bucket of potato salad that quickly emptied. The agents didn't hesitate to sit down for dinner.

Agent Phillips commented, "You don't know how many patty melts and burgers I have to eat. I'm not turning down a home cooked meal." It was odd for Bess to see the two G-Men, who normally looked stuffy and worried all the time, smiling and stuffing their faces. But her father's cooking was delicious.

After they ate, Portia said, "I'm certain you didn't come over hear because you smelled dinner on the grill."

"No," Agent Marsh answered, "We do have business. And I understand you had a bit of an adventure today, besides catching these fish," he pointed at the dwindling dolphin plate. "I wanted to ask you about what you saw today, and to show you your photos."

Bess looked over her shoulder. The strange camera that the agents had given them sat unceremoniously on a desk next to the radio. It's back had been removed where the film would have been. "I didn't think you wanted that left in the Starlighter so I brought it here," Steve said.

"We got the film when you took it back to the airport, and had it developed. I want to show you something," Agent Marsh pulled a folder out of a small satchel he had brought in. "First of all, this thing you saw, about how long was it?"

Bess pictured it in her head. It was hard to tell from that far away. "Maybe 60-80 feet." She thought about the size of the boat, then looked around the room at the size of the walls. The inside was about 40 feet wide, and what she saw wouldn't fit inside the house. "Yes, maybe 60 feet. It was pretty big."

Aurora agreed. "It was making waves that made it longer, but yes, 60 feet or so. It was huge."

Agent Marsh pulled out a set of photos. "You took ten pictures of the Soviet trawlers out there. Most of them showed nothing more than we already knew. They are working fishing ships. And they definitely have some spying capabilities. We can see these antennas here," he pointed at the bridge.

"But look at these pictures." He pulled out three of them. "Here is the first one. You can see this long box on the side, about the same length as your sea monster." He pointed at a gray rectangle like a shipping box. "Next to it, if you look close, you can see two sets of lines in the water." Two thin lines, ropes or cables, were taut into the calm seas next to the ship.

"Here is the next one," he said, holding out another large black and white photo. Where the ropes were the water had turned white, as if something large had been thrown in with a splash.

"And this one," he said.

On the side of the ship there was... something. A strange shadow, along with a small blob of black, hung over the ship. It obviously was connected to the lines, but it was as if nothing was there, almost. "What is that?" Bess asked.

"That's what we want to know," said Agent Phillips.

"Look at this," Agent Marsh continued. "We blew it up some, but we lose what little detail there is. We do get the basic shape of this shadow, or clear spot, whatever it is."

The shape was transparent, only visible as the sun was passing through it. "Whatever it is, these photos are in reverse order. They weren't recovering it. They were launching it."

Bess took the photo and looked closely, but couldn't make any detail out. Then, in a flash of recognition, she grabbed a pen and started to draw along the shadowy outline. The figure took shape slowly, first with a strange rounded point on the front, then triangles on the top and bottom. Finally, a narrow and tall shape at the end.

"What does that look like?" she whispered.

No one spoke, but everyone knew exactly what it was. The shape Bess had drawn looked exactly like that of a giant shark.

CHAPTER 14

Ghost Stroll

The image with a drawing over it kept everyone silent for a moment. It was a realization that they had even more questions, with no answers. Bess wondered if this strange... thing... had anything to do with the wrecked fishing boat, the appearance of all those sharks, and the tales of a sea monster out in the ocean. And more specifically, why was it doing these things? "What are the Russians up to?" she said slowly, out loud, but as much to herself as anyone else. She didn't expect an answer.

She wouldn't get one. "That's what we'd like to know," said Agent Marsh. "We had no idea they were testing anything around here."

"Well, now we know something," continued Agent Phillips. "We know what it looks like. A bit." He stared at the photo. "And, we can guess they may not be actually *testing* so much as *using*. But why they are, and what it does, those are answers we don't have."

Portia went over to a side table to gather a piece of cloth. Unwrapping it, she uncovered the strange crystal shape they found in the fishing boat. "We found this," she held it up, "and a few other broken pieces on that charter yacht that washed ashore last night. Jesse seems to have been correct when he said it looked like a shark's tooth. It just may not be a living shark."

"What's it made of?" asked Agent Marsh.

"That, I can't determine. I've done what I can here. I can only tell that it is extremely hard. This has no edge to scratch anything. Notice the curve at the point." She touched the end of the "tooth." "See how it is curved. This is similar to a tiger shark tooth, which I found in a book on fish in the library of the house. But it doesn't serve the same purpose. It may easily cut into something, but it is not sharp, not meant for tearing smaller fish."

Bess remembered the old fisherman telling them that sharks won't eat what they can't fit in their mouths. "This thing had a big mouth," she said.

"Indeed," said Agent Marsh, holding the photo.

Portia continued, waiting patiently for the group to focus back on her lecture. She knew that kids would easily be distracted, and let them run their imagination when they needed to. Especially now, she realized.

"Nothing short of a diamond will scratch it. I tested with a phonograph needle. It feels slightly light for its size, and has a slight blue tinge. My original suspicion is what I doubly believe now, but I still don't know how it can be true.

"I think it is is a type of man-made corundum, a type of aluminum that we know as sapphire."

"That's..." Lydia started the sentence that almost everyone was thinking. "That's impossible." No one could make mass quantities of a clear aluminum, nor a precious gemstone. But they all knew from what they had seen before, as well as the confidence that everyone had in Portia Truly's scientific skills, that if she said it was possible, then, there it was.

Only her husband Steve grinned at her. He was extremely proud of his wife's smarts.

"I'm not saying this is entirely a gemstone. I think it is some conglomerate, but I don't know how. Perhaps it is a step toward manufactured crystals, like the artificial ones used on chandeliers. It is some crystalline formation."

"So the Russians are out floating some strange transparent crystal shark?" said Aurora.

"Not crystal," Portia wanted to correct her own words, not Aurora. "Perhaps the best term would be hyaline, or crystalline."

"A hyaline shark," breathed Bess. "A sixty foot hyaline shark that attacks boats."

"I miss the desert," said Aurora defeatedly. "No sharks there."

"Yeah, I'll take the lizards any day," added Lydia.

The evening passed into night. While Bess's mother and father discussed the big issues of what the Russians would be doing with this strange hyaline shark just offshore, she and her friends wandered off to the sun deck facing the ocean. It looked different now. The delights of mystery hidden in the sea had changed for all of them.

"When I first got here," Bess reminisced, thinking of events of only a few days before as a lifetime ago, "the only thing I was curious about was that the house might be haunted. Then we worried about fish nibbling our toes. Then it was sharks. Now, this." The shark must be the cause of all these other problems, but the how and why were still hidden. Bess was used to facing problems head on. She had no idea how to fix this. It was so far out to sea.

"We're kids of the prairie," Aurora said. "I can ride a horse out, Jesse can drive his jalopy around, but one thing we can't do is float. No horse can swim that far," she pointed into the starry darkness offshore.

"Do you think those weird sounds we heard in the water were caused by the shark?" Lydia asked.

"I don't know if I want to go back out into the water now," Jesse exaggerated a wince as he rubbed the bandage over his arm.

Bess looked out over the nighttime ocean. She saw a few lights, red and green, of ships passing by far off to sea. The piers to the north and south were lit up for the fishermen. Her beach was a shadow of pitch black. She felt the concern, or was it fear, of walking out on the beach. If that shark was out there, could it churn its way up to shore, just walk up and take her and her friends to the cold depths?

No, she thought, that's nonsense. And Bess didn't like being afraid. She purposely set her foot into the sand and began walking down the low dune to the beach. "We won't find any clues to all this, but I'm sure I'm not going to let anyone or anything scare me off from the beach."

The others joined her, chasing the little ghost crabs and splashing in the shore break, until they were covered with sand and salt water. Tired but happy, the four walked back to the beach house to shower off and change.

Bess came inside, her hair wrapped around a rough worn towel, after showering off in the dark outside shower. "Jesse is right," she agreed as she spoke to her parents, "that shower is pretty keen. You don't track any sand into the house." Her strawberry blonde hair was darkened by the water, and twisted in tiny waves.

She noticed that agents Marsh and Phillips hadn't left yet. They were taking this very seriously, Bess could tell. "They must be talking with Mom about how the shark works," she thought.

"Hey, you know," she decided to mention the sounds she heard in the ocean, "when we were out swimming, we heard these weird noises under the water. We thought it maybe was a boat going by, but there were no boats out there. At least not that we saw."

"That's news to us," Agent Marsh said.

"Everything is news to us right now," Agent Phillips added. "We are learning as we go here."

"Do you know why the Russians are doing this?" Bess asked.

Agent Marsh was reluctant to share more with Bess. It was in his nature and business to keep secrets. But Bess already knew more than most people did, and they all knew she wouldn't share any secret information. Plus, she had experienced more of the shark than anyone else in the room. "We don't know the why, though we guess it is either a test or trial of technology, or perhaps they are looking to cause carnage and confusion. The Reds think different from us. It's a different world on their side."

"I think we need to focus upon the how, as in, how are they doing this, and how can we stop them," said Portia.

"I'm thinking we need to sleep on it, and get at it in the morning," added Steve, yawning. He had been up early and had a very long day. Warm food had put him in one of his fixed contented good moods, and not much would bring him down. He knew his wife would do the wondering. He was used to getting the orders and going out to do something, like he did in his fighter pilot days.

The agents took the hint. They bade the family goodnight, and left into the darkness. "I wonder where they are staying?" Bess said idly. "Or do you think they just stay up all night?" The two agents were mysterious, indeed.

Bess went upstairs to go to bed. Everyone was tired, but still excited about what they learned. She found Jesse tuning his new little transistor radio. The green and gray portable radio played a series of crooners and country music. Jesse, who worked at his father's radio station back in Three Winds, knew the singers by heart, and named them off. "That's George Hamilton IV," he said as the song *A Rose And A Baby Ruth* came on.

"I kind of like that," said Lydia. She usually liked the rocking sounds of Elvis Presley and Gene Vincent, but the soft ballad helped her close her eyes and start to nod off. The soft static and soft music filled the warm, stuffy upstairs while the open windows let in a salty bit of breeze and the gentle crash of waves on the nearby shore. They turned the lights off and climbed into their beds with the doors open to let the breeze blow through.

Bess felt herself grow tired. Her lids drooped, but her mind still raced with thoughts about ghosts and sharks and shipwrecks. She wondered if ghost pirates would sail by on the wind, chasing a silver clad shark for their illicit treasure.

Bess had strange and worrisome dreams that night. She tossed in the bed, kicking the sheets off to let the cooler ocean air blow through the windows. Some time in the middle of the night, she awoke to hear soft thumps from downstairs. The ghost was awake in the old beach house. Bess was too tired to even move. She wasn't able to focus enough to get up and see it. She hoped the ghost would clean up dishes in the kitchen. Quietly. Then go back to bed like any sensible ghost would. She turned over and fell back into a fitful sleep.

The whole house slept heavy, like the sleep of the dead. Early the next morning, the house would be almost completely quiet. Bess had chosen her bedroom because one window faced the ocean and eastern horizon. It was a strange and glorious sight to her when she would look out and see the morning sun just cracking over the flat ocean. It was a boiling orange ball that rose up into a purple sky. The little stars twinkled in the heavens, but couldn't compete with the bright piercing rays of the morning sun.

Bess awoke, stretched her arms, and sat up to see the sun begin to shine through her window. She breathed deeply, expecting the usual salt air with a tinge of sea. It was a fishy smell she was happily becoming used to. This breath was a little different.

Like someone was cooking bacon, but not good bacon. It was like a campfire burning with rags, not the good wood smell.

It was like a fire... her nose, her senses tried to awake her still sleeping brain.

It was like a fire, she heard something deep in her head say.

Bess jumped out of bed and ran toward the stairs. Smoke was already pouring up from the ceiling below.

"Fire!" Bess screamed. "The house is on fire!"

CHAPTER 15

A Fiery Escape

"Fire!" Bess screamed again. She had to get everyone up. She felt suddenly awake and overstimulated. Her body ached with the stress of the sudden change from sleep to alertness. She ran to the first room she could, Jesse's bedroom.

"Jesse, get up, the house is on fire!" Jesse jumped up, stunned by the words, and staggered around the room, still half asleep. He slammed his foot into the leg of the bed, "Aarrgh!" he cried, hopping on one foot.

Bess knew Jesse was in pain, but he was awake. She ran to the back of the upstairs, where Aurora and Lydia had their tiny rooms. "Wake up! The house is on fire! We have to get out!" She shook Aurora awake, who immediately sprung up out of her bed. "Who is up? Can we get out downstairs?"

Bess didn't answer, but barged through Aurora's room to the connecting door to the tiny room in the back that Lydia used. "Lydia," Bess saw her friend already waking from all the yelling, "get up, there's a fire downstairs."

Lydia sprang up and ran with Bess back out. They met Aurora and Jesse at the top of the stairs. Smoke began to billow up from the ceiling into the upstairs, but the air was still just clear enough to see down. "Let's go!" she quickly ran down the steps. "We have to get my parents up!"

Downstairs, they looked around. Bess ran to the front bedroom and woke her parents, who were sound asleep in the bed. Bess shook her mother, always a deep sleeper, while her father was up in a second. He responded to danger quickly as part of his training as a pilot.

"There's a fire!" Bess yelled.

"Where?" Steve asked as he grabbed at a t-shirt.

Jesse ran in, "There's a fire on the porches," he exclaimed. "Right outside the doors."

They ran to the living room and looked at the front and back doors. Flames were bouncing up against the windows, making terrifying streaks in the old glass. Fingers of fire danced and teased at the outside of the house, as if they were drumming on the doors and walls to be let in so they could continue their damage.

The rear door already had the outside screen door on fire, and smoke leaked in from the wide cracks of the old house.

"What do we do?" cried Lydia.

"Back upstairs?" suggested Jesse. "We can go out a window and jump?"

"No," said Portia, her mind working even if her body was still half asleep. "The porch roofs would be directly over the fire. Maybe another window?" She looked around.

"Wait!" Bess called out. Then she ran to the center of the living room and grabbed the rug. "The trap door! Everyone, move, help me get this rug!" The group scattered to corners and picked up the rug. They threw it unceremoniously against a wall, exposing the trap door.

Bess grabbed the little recessed handle, just an old circular ring, and pulled. The door came up easily, and a rush of cool shaded air, clean and without smoke, cleared their heads.

Pushing Jesse first, then Aurora, she shouted to them, "Go that way, knock down the fence under the house." The old beach house had wood slats under it. Jesse and Aurora crawled their way through the soft cool sand and began to kick at the old wood.

"Lydia go, Mom, you're next," Bess insisted. She pushed her mother, while her father guided Portia to jump down. Father and daughter knew that Portia might argue about Bess going next, so they gave her no choice. Bess jumped down next. She saw Lydia already pulling Portia to the opening that Aurora had made.

A splash of sand hit Bess as her father joined her and started crawling on his hands and knees in the low underside of the house. "C'mon, kiddo, we're not out of the fight yet." He encouraged Bess to move, but didn't grab at her. He knew Bess would be moving as fast as possible.

The entire group made their way safely out the side of the house. Steve immediately ran to the front to get the hose and begin spraying down the front porch. Jesse had disappeared. Bess found him scooping up sand into a big tin bucket, and then throwing it on the fire by the door. It seemed like a hopeless task, but he was still going to try.

Bess looked around, but found nothing to use to help fight the flames. Aurora ran around the house to join them. She, too, looked for something to gather sand to throw on the fire. Jesse was already getting hot, sweaty and tired. It took him so long to gather sand that he made no progress. Aurora's face lit up as she ran to the outdoor shower. Just beside it was an old wide pail of water that they used to rinse their feet off. She grabbed the heavy bucket to carry up the stairs to the porch where she threw the water and muddy contents at the base of the flaming door. The flames sizzled and shrunk with a huge cloud of thick steam, but then they came back to continue to beat at the back door.

The screen door had come completely off and was laying on the burning porch, a charred frame of peeling paint and black wood.

Lydia came to the back to help, too. "Should we go back in and get our stuff out?" she yelled. "Everything we have is in there." In the rush to escape, they only had shorts and t-shirts. Jesse wore his old beach shorts and a dirty undershirt. It was already stained from the ash, soot, and smoke.

"No!" Bess insisted. Fires were rare at her ranch back home, but they happened occasionally. There was always a worry of a fire in a barn or stable. It had been instilled in her from an early age to get out from a fire, not go in. Nothing that wasn't alive was worth going back for.

"All our clothes," Lydia sighed. She felt hopeless, unable to join in to help fight the flames, and she couldn't go back in to get anything, either.

Then, in a flash, Lydia had a realization. She ran toward the old carriage house where the Jeep was parked inside. They had rarely used the vehicle since they had been there, but Lydia remembered one thing. Without slowing, she barged hard into the big plywood door to the back of the garage. It cracked, splintered, and then gave way. Lydia stumbled but stayed on her feet as she disappeared into the dark garage.

Bess and Aurora watched, dumbfounded, seeing their best friend, who worried about her clothes and hair, who was worried about sharks and crabs at the beach, break a door to splinters. Before either could react, Lydia came storming back out, carrying a long silver cylinder.

Lydia found a fire extinguisher that had been attached to the old Willys truck. She was the only one that remembered it was there. Lydia ran up the stairs with it, pulled the pin and aimed the hose at the base of the flames.

A white blast of CO_2 and sodium bicarbonate poured out over the flames, suffocating the monster right at its source. Lydia sprayed the extinguisher contents liberally over each spot of fire until there were large piles of white powder over any hint of the fire. She kept spraying even after the fire was out.

"I think you got it," Jesse commented as he stared at the furious girl who fought the fire and won. He looked at her like he didn't recognize Lydia.

"It's not going to do any good in the can," Lydia answered, and kept laying down the smothering powder. It took her a few moments to catch herself. She slowed, then stopped. Lydia dropped the can and fairly staggered to the back steps to sit down. Her body went from excited to exhausted as her small frame had just hauled the heavy tank around to put out the fire.

Jesse didn't say anything, but he picked up the extinguisher and ran to the front of the house in case Steve needed it. The front didn't seem to have been as bad as the back.

"Wowzers!" Aurora threw down her pail of water, "You really got your berries razzed, Lydia!"

"Don't ever go after this girl's clothes!" joked Bess as she sat down near her.

"Ugh!" Lydia looked at herself. She always liked having her hair and clothes perfect. Now she was dirty, covered with ash and bits of white powder. Her shorts were still caked with paint and wood from when she broke down the door to the garage. Her sleep shirt, a delicate white with lace ruffles on the sleeves, was gray from smoke. "I'm a mess."

Aurora sat next to her. She pushed a strand of hair out of her exhausted and scared friend's face. "Don't worry. You're still a dolly. Always will be." Aurora hugged her friend.

Behind them, a tiny flame began to flicker from the remnants of the fire. Lydia jumped up and grabbed a sandy rag mat from the steps. She swung at the flame mercilessly, screaming at it, "Get bent!" She beat at the fire without remorse until it, too, was out.

Jesse came back around the corner, slowing as he saw Lydia scream. He stopped in his tracks.

Lydia, breathing heavily, saw a lap of fire, no bigger than a finger, a weak attempt to burn, do a tiny dance. She stared at it, then said, menacingly, "No you don't, nosebleed!" The fire withered and died with her stare.

Jesse stopped in his tracks, put up his hands, and slowly backed away.

CHAPTER 16

Mystery Ride

It was all over by the time the fire trucks showed up. They were only a mile down the road, but had little to do except douse the smelly embers with water to make sure it was out. The firefighters stood around idly. They wanted to make sure no flames were still hiding in the soaked wood.

"Boy, Mac is going to be mad," Steve said. Normally he wore a near permanent smile, but the fire and danger to his family had put a frown on his handsome face. His pilot friend would have to be told about the fire.

"Wonder what started it?" Jesse looked around at the wood porches, now disheveled from the pressure of the fire hoses.

"I wonder why it started," said Bess. "How does a fire start in two places at once?"

"It's lucky you knew about that trap door," said Aurora. "We would have been jumping out of the top floor windows if you didn't."

"Or worse," said Lydia. The rest were silent. They didn't want to comment on what could have happened.

The fire chief came over. "It looks like the fires started from some mats placed by the doors." He held up charred remains of two rolled mats, made of twisted rags tied together. "Any of you smoke? I found burnt matches by each of them."

Everyone shook their heads. No one in the house smoked.

"It wasn't the grill was it?" Steve suddenly had the realization that he had been cooking outside in the back.

"No," said the chief, "that was one of the first things we checked. You had that in the right place, away from the house, not under or near anything. It is still there, and cold. It looked like you soaked what little charcoal you had left in water."

Steve nodded his head in agreement. He had put out any heat from the grill long before they went to bed.

"You know," Bess said wonderingly, "last night, I woke up. I heard something downstairs. Honestly, I thought it was the ghost." She smiled, embarrassed, "or maybe just Dad up. I was too tired to get up and see."

"You think someone came in and set the fire?" asked the chief. "But why?"

Bess kept her mouth closed. Some of the events were just too secret to reveal. "No, I doubt that, Maybe it was just the ghost."

"It could have been a prank," said the chief, "but if it was, it was a mighty bad one." He had seen trouble like this on occasion before, but it was usually just unoccupied sheds on the dunes where people started campfires. "We'll tell the police to investigate."

Once it was safe, they all went inside to gather their things. They would stay at a nearby hotel for the rest of the vacation. Bess kept wondering, "Who would want to set the house on fire, and endanger all of us?" As they gathered their clothes, Bess thought of something.

She ran down the stairs and looked at the table where the big radio sat, now silent. Fortunately, nothing inside had been damaged. She looked around the table, and saw it was empty.

The photos of the Russian trawler, and the hyaline shark, were gone.

By noon the fire had become local news, with the story passing along the local person to person telegraph of the islands. Jesse and Lydia had taken the Jeep with all their clothes to a nearby laundromat to wash out any smoke smell. Her mother and father stood separate from her and Aurora, talking in conspiratorial and worried tones. They now knew that someone had come into the beach house late that night, stolen the photos, and then set fire to the house to cover their tracks.

Bess's parents were relieved when their new friend Vicki showed up on horseback. "Wow, a fire!" she said it like *farr*, with her soft Outer Banks accent. Bess told her the short version of the story, leaving out the more secret details. "Where you staying?" Vicki asked.

"That new hotel down there," Bess pointed. "The Sea Foam. It looks nice."

"Hey, you know, why don't you come stay with me tonight? We can go camping out in the woods. You wanted to see some ghosts? Well, we can go ghost hunting! Shoot, I can even round us up horses for us all to ride."

It sounded wonderful to Bess. She missed her horse, Electra, and definitely could use some time riding instead of thinking about all that had happened in the past few days. She hadn't had the time to explore the other parts of the island yet. When she mentioned it to her parents, they immediately approved.

Jesse drove the girls out to Vicki's home in the woods in the Jeep. He decided to go back to the beach house and help clean up. Jesse preferred to drive his jalopy to riding a horse when he was back home. "I still need to send Annie a postcard. I haven't had a chance to get one yet." Annie was his girlfriend back in Three Winds.

Bess, Aurora, and Lydia met Vicki's parents at their house on the west side of the island. They lived in an older home. Vicki explained that people used to only live on this side of the Outer Banks, because the beach was so rough when storms hit, and was always windy. Here, the trees sheltered the houses, and provided places to hunt and fish. Bess looked around at the forest that surrounded her. She hadn't seen this many trees in her life.

In between the trees were wide black pools of fresh water, and ferns and orchids grew plentifully. Bugs were everywhere, singing and buzzing in the overgrowth. If Bess was ever told there would be a thick maritime forest on a sandy island, just a few miles from her beach house, she would never have believed it, until she saw it just now.

"You all know how to ride, right?" Vicki asked. "We have two horses, but our neighbor has several. They can let us use a couple for you." She was delighted to show off her home to the visitors.

After getting the horses saddled, Vicki led them out along an old road of clay and dust. "This used to be to only road out here. Nothing over on the beach side. It goes all the way up past the Wright Brothers Monument into Kitty Hawk."

The road, almost just a trail, wound around hills and overgrown cliffs that the girls couldn't believe existed on such a flat place. The heat of the day filtered through the canopy of leaves. Mosquitoes and biting flies came out when they smelled the horses and riders.

"Let's go back for lunch, then come out when it's cooler. You'll love this place in the evening. I'll even show you where the ghosts are," Vicki teased.

They waited until near twilight to go riding again. Coated with bug spray and long pants, Bess was more comfortable in her regular riding clothes of jeans and a long sleeve shirt, even if it was still warm. An evening breeze blew in fast from the sound side. The shallow water had tiny lapping waves, and a decidedly musty scent, much different from the salt spray of the ocean.

"Ride up here," Vicki insisted. Bess, Aurora, and Lydia followed the girl and her sure footed horse up a narrow path, before stopping at an open spot cleared out of the rolling hills. Several tombstones sat at different angles in the yellow silty clay ground.

"This used to be where the old church was. It burned down years ago. There's still the old graves. Lots of old cemeteries all over this area. They say..." she paused for effect, "that the graves were so shallow, the bodies could come right back up. That the ghosts still walk around in these woods." She looked around as if checking behind the trees for emphasis.

The other girls giggled with delight. They hadn't been in a place so thick with trees and brush like this before, and adding ghosts wandering around, just beyond the boundary of an old abandoned cemetery, made the night time exploration even more deliciously frightening.

"C'mon," encouraged Vicki, "I know where we may see some ghosts. We may even make it to the old haunted house."

Vicki led the group up and down some low hills, as Bess and her friends walked with their Zap-Guns pointed out, providing a soft but full light to the night. "Okay," said Vicki at nearly a whisper, "turn those ray gun things off, and watch."

The woods got dark, then, as the girls got used to the nighttime, they began to see better. Stars were intensely bright, and somewhere through the trees a bit of moonlight filtered. The first strange sight happened so softly, they barely noticed.

"What was that?" Lydia barely whispered. She wasn't sure if she said it to herself.

"Wait," commanded Vicki.

Then, another flash of flight, soft and wavy, appeared over a dark pond hidden in the low spot of the woods. It flickered, then danced. Strange blue flames perked up over the water, and slowly floated across the inky surface. Bess felt Lydia squirm, and Aurora leaned forward against her.

The blue light turned into a ball, with strange tentacles swimming off into the air. For a few moments, little versions seemed to peel off and float, only to disappear into a humid and black ether of the night.

"What *is* that?" Bess broke the silence with more effort than Lydia's soft appeal. If it was a ghost, it was nothing like the legends and tales of spooky apparitions wearing white sheets. This was a strange ball of light that appeared out of nowhere.

"It's foxfire, will-o'-the-wisp," Vicki whispered back, as if to keep from scaring it off. "It's like a gas or something that comes up from the old stuff underground, and it lights up and glows at night. No one really knows why."

With those words, the strange light twisted in a dance and vanished.

"C'mon," Vicki encouraged them, "Let's go see the haunted house."

The girls were intrigued. They had been promised a ghost, and Vicki had delivered. They had seen an old abandoned cemetery and then a floating blue figure over a black lake. That was about as close as they could get to a real ghost adventure. "No one is going to believe us when we get home," Aurora said.

"I still don't believe it, and I saw it," Lydia retorted.

"I wonder what we'll see at this haunted house," Bess added.

They didn't have to wait long. Vicki led them to an old drive, overgrown with wild plants on each side of a cut through the sand hill. "This place is old. It's been around since the 1800s, easy. No one has been in it for years, not since I was born. It's always empty. Just the ghosts live there."

They walked out into an open area at the base of a rising hill. On top was an old, old house. It looked a little like the houses on the beach, with a wide porch and overhanging shades on the windows. It was two stories tall, on top of low pilings. If it ever had a lick of paint, every bit had probably blown off in the storms and hurricanes over the decades.

All the windows were black as can be. No light shone from the house.

Except at the top. One window glowed a soft warm light through a curtain. The veil cut the light down to almost nothing. The light would probably not make it even to the road behind Bess and the other girls.

"That's strange," said Vicki, slowly walking up the drive to the house, "I never seen that light be..."

They saw something move behind the light, a shadow of a figure lurking in the room.

Then the front door opened.

CHAPTER 17

A Ghostly Theft

From the safety of the twisted bushes and tree branches, Bess watched as a dark figure held the door open, waiting for someone else to come out. Then two if them walked down the steps and to the side of the house. In moments, a car started. Bess froze, worried that her motion might make her seen.

"No one should be in that place," Vicki said. "It's been abandoned for years." She almost stood up to confront the driver, but Lydia rested a soft hand on the other girl's arm.

No, wait," Lydia insisted. "Let's wait until the car is gone."

They watched as the white car drove down the sandy drive, then disappear on the old Nags Head Woods road, toward Jockey's Ridge.

"Did that car look familiar?" Bess asked. In the dark, she couldn't make out details, especially with the bright lights shining toward her. It was just an older white car.

"It's pretty plain looking," Aurora said. "Could be anybody. Did you see who was driving? They look like anyone you know?" She directed the last question to Vicki.

"Nope. Like I said, no one should be there."

"Let's go see what they are doing," Bess said. She stared up at the room on the top of the house. The moon was coming up past the trees now, and it shone onto the upstairs room. The light was still dim behind a curtain, but no shadows moved. Bess hoped that the two people were the only ones in the house, and that they had both left. She stared up at the window, then noticed something above it, on the roof.

Through the moonlight, a strange web of metal protruded. "Look at that TV antenna," Bess commented. "I've never seen one like that before." It looked like a curved net or mesh, with a pole sticking out of the middle.

"What if someone else is there?" Lydia asked.

"We could just go up and knock," Vicki suggested. "If no one comes to the door, we know it's empty."

"People in dark houses that should be empty generally aren't who you want to meet at the door," Aurora joined in.

"Let's just go up quietly, and look in," Bess decided.

Bess and her friends had done their share of exploring, and knew how to be quiet. They wouldn't even utter a whisper or a *sshh* as they walked. Vicki had no choice but to go along. She wanted to see what was happening in the house, anyway. She didn't like people sneaking around her neighborhood.

Bess walked slowly around the house, looking for ways in and out, besides the front door. The back opened to the woods, while the front with the dirt drive led toward the clay road and the sound waters past it. Bess waved to Aurora to watch for the car coming back. In the dark, its headlights should be easy to spot.

Bess looked in a back window. She could see only a little by the light of the moon, but didn't want to shine a light inside just yet. She could see a table and chairs, and beyond that, deeper into the dark room, a set of metal boxes.

And what looked like a microphone.

Lydia and Vicki walked up silently next to her, peering in. "Doesn't look like anyone is there," Vicki broke the silence. It was aching at her not to talk. A few words would help break the tension.

"Look," Lydia whispered. She pointed at the edge of the table with the boxes.

"Yeah, it looks like a radio," Bess whispered back. "That's what that antenna is for."

"No!" Lydia was insistent. "On the table," she pointed again.

Sitting on the edge were some papers. On top was a camera.

"That's my camera!" Bess almost spoke out loud. She looked around in the darkness to see if she had been discovered, but the land was as empty as a graveyard. And just as quiet.

She walked to the back door and tried the doorknob. It was loose but still locked. She jiggled it to see if the lock would give, but the door wouldn't open. Bess pulled her Zap-Gun from its holster. "I'm getting my camera back and finding out who these people are."

With a twist of the barrel, and a quick spin on the power dial, she held the barrel at the old key hole and shot a tiny purple spark into the lock. It popped and fizzed, then clinked. The knob spun open freely.

Bess walked in with Lydia, while Vicki watched outside. All of them were scared, but they also didn't like knowing that someone was in the house without permission, and they were the ones that stole Bess's camera.

Bess went over and picked it up. Under the camera were several documents and plans. In the darkness, she couldn't see what they were, but something looked familiar. Risking more noise and light, she turned her Zap-Gun down to the lowest setting and barely squeezed the trigger. A soft blue glow came out onto the emitter, lighting up the papers.

Bess couldn't read the weird writing on it. The printing was soft and poor, like it was a badly made copy, but the image was clear.

It was exactly the same shape as the hyaline shark.

"Get out your Zap-Gun," Bess told Lydia. "Hold it over these papers. Give me a little light."

Lydia lit up the documents with a soft glow from her own Zap-Gun. Bess took her camera and held it steady, tight to her head, as she took photos of the paper under the low light. The camera shutter snapped slowly. Bess worried she would either shake the camera or there wasn't enough light to even capture the images. She hurried through, not willing to risk the time she really needed to take.

"Just a couple more," Bess insisted as she thumbed across the papers.

In that moment, a soft flash came from the front yard. It caught everyone's attention. They looked up through the front windows and doors. Far off, a car's headlights were coming through the trees. It was eerie, as the lights filtered like ghosts through the branches. The car was silent from inside the house.

"That's them," Vicki hissed from the door. "Let's get out of here!"

Bess wanted to see who they were, but didn't want to endanger their new friend.

"Wait," Lydia insisted, "If you take the camera, they'll know we were here!"

Bess thought for a moment, then snapped her fingers. "I got it!" she said, then began winding the film back up into its canister. She snapped the camera open, popped out the 35mm film, and placed it in her pocket. Then she carefully set the camera back on top of the papers. "Let's beat feet!"

The three of them ran quickly out the back door, pulling it closed. Bess hoped they wouldn't notice the broken lock, or think the old door just gave out. They ran to the protection of the dark woods as the car turned into the long drive at the front of the house.

"What about Aurora?!" Vicki asked in fear.

"She knows what to do," Bess assured her. "This isn't her first rodeo. She'll know to hide and then look for us on the road to your house. We'll meet her there. Just get us to the road without being seen."

Vicki was unsure as to what to do. She had seen older kids come up into the woods. Mostly they caused trouble for the hunters and fishermen who came for some peace and quiet, or left trash from their parties and campfires. This was different. It felt much more dangerous. She wasn't sure what she had gotten into.

But Bess and Lydia seemed to know what they were doing. Even in a strange and dark place, they were confident and assured. They moved quietly and with purpose around the house. They were far enough away that they wouldn't be seen or heard, and moved quickly even in complete darkness. Vicki stepped forward to find a small deer trail she knew was nearby. She waved to them, then took Bess's hand. Bess in turn held Lydia's as the three walked single file in a low crouch out of the thick woods toward the twisty and open road.

Now to their left and farther away, they could see the car come to a stop at the house. The lights turned off and the house was in complete darkness. Even the light from the top room was blotted out by leaves on the tall trees.

"Aurora will start moving now," Bess said matter-of-factly. "Let's get to a spot where she can find us."

They moved more quickly now. They were less worried about being seen. It would be a hot and sweaty run back to the comfort of Vicki's house, but it was also a place of relative safety. They were more confident with every step. Soon they came to a clearing where the road was. It was lit by the light of the moon, with the canopy of trees cleared enough to see the beat up one lane dirt path. "Let's wait here," Bess said. "We can see down the road, but this little curve gives us a hiding spot in case any cars come by."

Waiting in the darkness was always agonizingly long. Bess felt something tickle her neck. It was a bug, or a drop of sweat, but she couldn't bring herself to swat at it with her hand. She just embraced the dark and dirty night, knowing she could clean up later. "I've been through worse," Bess thought, honestly.

It might have felt like an hour, but in a minute in real time, a dark figure came running at high speed down the road. Bess recognized the figure of her friend Aurora in a beat of her pounding heart. Slight gasps came from her direction, and a bouncy ponytail swished, black on black, as her raven hair waved in the darkness. "That's her," Bess said.

Suddenly, from farther away came a loud crashing sound. And lights appeared again in the woods. The car was going out from the house, and this time it was speeding away. The rough crunch of spinning tires of dirt and gravel, along with a revving engine, gave away the desperation of the driver.

Then the lights turned their way.

Bess thought fast, then yelled out, "Aurora, quick, around the turn, as fast as you can."

Aurora, only a dark wraith of a figure, began to run at tremendous speed. She was a natural athlete, and could run both long distances and incredibly fast sprints. The noise of the car coming her way added a sense of desperation to her already fast moving feet.

"C'mon, move!" Bess begged. She had only one shot at this.

The car rounded the far curve. Its light shone brightly down the dirt road. Right onto Aurora, running away as fast as she could.

The engine revved louder as the car increased speed.

CHAPTER 18

Danger In The Pieces

The car was bearing down on Aurora, who only had moments to reach Bess at the curve in the road. The car skidded in a patch of soft sand, giving her welcomed seconds to escape the charging vehicle.

"C'mon, *run!*" Bess insisted. The car's headlights wobbled side to side in the dark, spurring Aurora on even faster. Bess stood in the woods, up a small hill from the road, with the other girls. "I'm going to stop the car. When Aurora gets past here, go get her, and head to your home, fast."

Aurora flew across the road. The tight curve allowed her to disappear from view for a moment, which also gave Bess time to go to work. As soon as Aurora passed, Bess pulled her Zap-Gun out from its holster, quickly dialed it up to high, and pointed at a large tree leaning over the road. The dark branches were already frightening in the dark night, like a bony hand dripping inky blackness over the sandy clay road. "I hope this works," Bess said to herself.

She triggered the Zap-Gun at close range toward the trunk of the tree. The thick living wood gave way begrudgingly, with lots of chips and splinters shooting out toward her. Bess had carved a hole into the base of the tree, but the solid wood held. She continued to pour on the electricity until the trunk finally gave way. It was cut open like a wide mouth at the base. The tree began to tumble as it fell down from the hill.

The old white car had just reached the curve when the tree came down. The sight must have panicked the driver. The car was put into a slide, then a soft skid. The engine revved while the tires made a sifting growl in the loose clay. It banged into the hill, then bounced back into the road.

The tree crashed down right across the car's hood and windshield. It stopped immediately as it got wedged under the thick broken branches.

Bess ran up the hill, into darkness. Then she decided to double back. The car wasn't going anywhere. She knew Aurora and her friends had escaped into the woods, and would be near Vicki's house soon. Bess found a spot to stare out at the car from the safety of the woods.

She saw two figures get out, but couldn't discern any features with the white glare of the headlights.

Steam poured from the hood. The driver banged on the roof, obviously angered by the situation.

Bess listened. She could hear them talk, but couldn't make out what they were saying, even though they spoke with obvious emotion and anger.

The words seemed muffled in the thick air. "Vy pozvolili im uyti!" screamed the passenger. His voice was deep, guttural.

"Eto nichego ne menyayet. oni nichego ne znayut. My pozabotimsya o tom, chtoby im nechego bylo nayti, i nashi plany ne menyayutsya!" The driver answered. The voice almost sang, with a beautiful lilt, full of confidence. Bess saw the slim figure, surprised that the person chasing Aurora down was probably a young woman. She had no idea what they were saying.

They got back into the car. The engine revved and wheels screamed as it backed its way out from under the tree that blocked the road. It chugged and protested, but was somehow able to back up and then disappear into the night.

Bess hurried back to Vicki's house.

It would take hours and hours to finally begin to understand what was happening. Bess, Aurora, and Lydia all had to go back to the motel. Jesse showed up in the Jeep to take them back. Even in the open back seat, with the summer wind blowing on them, the girls found the ride relaxing after their adventure. Aurora propped her feet on the front passenger seat from her place in the back. Lydia let her hair out as she leaned over the side, letting the rushing wind twist and tangle her curls. Bess continued to pick splinters and bits of wood from her clothes and hair. Jesse kept his eyes on the road, with a twisted smile on his face. He had missed the excitement, but from where he sat, that probably was a good thing.

Bess's parents knew how to contact the G-Men. Agents Marsh and Phillips came to question the girls. When Bess presented her roll of film, it created another difficult situation. There was no place on the islands to develop it. Phillips got into his car and drove the film to a military base an hour away. It was an agonizing wait.

By the time they had the pictures, the sun was already coming up. Bess slept fitfully, first in a chair, then finally on the bed in her hotel room. Lydia and Aurora had long ago given in to sleep in an adjoining room, where they slept the sleep of the dead. Bess went back to her room and showered when Agent Phillips showed up with the developed photos. They included several enlargements the size of a letter.

When Bess came back over to her parents' room, they were already pouring over the photos. Agent Marsh looked up with a serious look on his face as she opened the door. He pointedly moved his hand down from his suit jacket.

"Maybe I should have knocked first," Bess half joked. The looks on the other faces in the room were all focused, their bodies tight and jumpy.

"Look at this," Portia turned back to the photos of the plans. "This is definitely what Bess photographed from the Starlighter." It was a blueprint line drawing of a shark, of sorts. There were no details that would be found on a real animal, but it did have the same basic look. "I don't know much about sharks, but I don't think this a shark. I wish I could read this writing."

"Hey, I know about sharks," Jesse came in, startling everyone.

"Maybe we should lock that door," Bess said.

"Why bother?" her father asked, "The rest of your crew of Zap-Gun Rangers are fast asleep."

"What's up with a shark?" Jesse asked, wanting to get back to a subject he liked. "I have been reading up on them."

Portia held up the picture for Jesse to look at. "Okay, so this thing, well it's got the pectoral fins," he pointed at the two fins on the bottom of the shark, behind the jaw, "and its dorsal, that's the one that cuts through the water, though sharks rarely do that, really, unless it's shallow. There's the keel, but that looks really thick," he noted the wide part that attached the tail to the trunk of the shark, "and that's the tail, of course. It's pretty big, too."

He looked closer. "But those don't look like gills. And it's missing the second set of fins here," he pointed again at the thick keel. "And I don't know *what* that stuff is," he pointed at a large dark shape in the middle of the shark. "Sharks have big, long livers, to help them swim. They wouldn't be shaped like that. It looks more like an engine, really. Like an old Ford Flathead."

"These look like labels," Steve was looking at the words on the paper, "but I can't read these at all. Not any language I know.

"You don't think this is..." he paused, then continued, "more of *you-know-who* from *you-know-where*?" He looked up while pointing at the ceiling.

"No, it's not our new friends, but more likely some of our older ones," answered Agent Marsh.

"Can you read this?" Portia asked. As a scientist, she read multiple languages, and spoke fluent Spanish and English.

Steve stared at the weird writing. He, too, spoke several languages, not nearly as well as his wife. "It looks familiar. But my German was never very good, and I haven't spoken French in years."

"It's not German, French, or Spanish, that's for sure," Marsh replied. "That's Cyrillic."

Bess gasped. "You mean, this is the Russkies?!"

"Likely."

"Can you translate it?" Portia was now focused on learning what the "shark" did.

"It will be tough," Agent Marsh said. "We can understand it, but translating Cyrillic is difficult. It is written differently than spoken."

Bess looked at the words. They used shapes she recognized, but some were turned around backwards, and others looked like numbers.

Agent Marsh seemed to give in with dejection. Things were taking too long. His partner then had a revelation. He snapped his fingers and picked up the phone, "We have to risk it," he said cryptically. Marsh seemed to agree, and then he hurriedly rushed everyone from the room to the outside porch. "It's probably better if you didn't hear this," he just said.

Phillips came out a few minutes later. With a nod to Marsh, he said, "I found a Navy guy. He's coming up now. Be here in a little over an hour."

Another agonizing wait came over the group. By this time, Aurora and Lydia had woken up. They put on their swimsuits and sat by the pool. The morning sun already warmed them. The girls enjoyed the change of climate. The air was thick, humid, and full of salt spray. Once it warmed up, they jumped into the crystal blue waters of the pool to cool off.

Bess couldn't relax. She eyed her parents as they stood outside the door to their room with the two G-Men. Her father leaned casually on the wall, while her mother paced in short steps. Marsh looked at his watch every ten seconds, and Phillips hiked his pants every time he looked up and down the parking lot, as if a car would show up any minute. It would be a lot of "any minutes" before a white military truck pulled up about an hour and a half later. A young but stern looking sailor got out. He barely looked any older than Jesse, Bess thought. He had short cropped blond hair and blotchy pale skin that was emphasized by his crisp white uniform. He also carried a seriousness in his walk, with stiff shoulders and a sharp salute to Agents Marsh and Phillips. The two waited for him to put his hand down, then politely shook his hand. They took the young man inside.

Bess glanced around, looking for people wondering what was happening. She worried she would start seeing spies and saboteurs everywhere now. A family with little kids came out of a room, dragging floats and chairs. Bess almost laughed at the thought that they were Russian spies. Then she thought, they would be the best spies, because no one would believe they were spies.

She could get paranoid thinking like this.

Then she remembered what had happened to them the night before.

About ten minutes later, the sailor came out. Bess ran over to see her mother, to find out what they had found out. Portia couldn't blame her for being curious.

Agent Marsh opened the door again, and called for Portia to come inside. Steve joined her. The agents didn't consider telling him to wait. There was no way they could stop him from being with his wife. With a look and a slight smile, Agent Phillips grinned at Bess, "Well? You might as well. You already know everything else."

Inside, Portia looked over the translation. "These words, *remote receiver*, and *short transceiver*, both show some sort of radio remote control, as well as the ability to send signals. This," she pointed to another translation, "*hydraulic propulsion* and *forced tunnel drive*, must have to do with how the thing moves. It looks like it is propelled like a water jet, and steered via the tail, which may explain why the keel that Jesse noticed is so thick. It needs to be to have more controls in it."

Portia frowned at another translation. The photo showed the shark's mouth, as well as what looked like part of the propulsion. "I'd say this is part of that tunnel drive propulsion, but..." her words slowly trailed away.

Portia got up and went to her suitcase. She opened a cloth inside and opened it to display the crystal shark's tooth they recovered from the shipwreck of the fishing yacht. "Oh.. my dear..." Portia spoke gravely. Her thoughts were obviously shaking her.

"Look at this shape," she said, pointing out the curve of the tooth. "It's not just a flat curve. It hooks, making something more like... a cup, or... honestly, I don't know the word in English. It's like a *cesta*, a curved basket, like a crescent moon. See, here?" she pointed to the interior of the tooth.

"What does that matter?" asked Agent Marsh. He was getting worried now, too.

"This diagram, this doesn't drive the water out the propulsion system of the shark to move it.

"See here? This translates to something like hydraulic surge.

"This pushes water out the front of the shark. With the size of the shark, and the figures here, it's like getting hit with a jet engine filled with water." Portia tried to grasp the power the diagram was showing.

"It would create an immensely powerful water surge, one that can be focused and directed with great intensity."

Bess realized what her mother was saying. "You mean... it could focus the water into a small area, but then create...

"a tidal wave?!"

CHAPTER 19

Mystery Signals

Things started happening rapidly after everyone had figured out what was going on with the strange hyaline shark. Little of the discoveries did much good, as they left Bess, her family, friends, and the agents with more questions and no real answers.

Marsh and Phillips had gone to the old haunted house later that day, only to find it had burned down to ash. The building was old, made of local wood that was unpainted. It made for a destructive kindling that let the house go up in flames so quickly that the fire had no ability to reach the nearby trees in the old woods. There was no sign of the radio in the charred remains. "We think they must have taken it with them," said Agent Marsh, "then soaked the house in an accelerant to have it burn quickly. The fire department didn't even know it was burning until the fire had consumed the whole place. We won't find anything there."

Bess's family decided to move back over to the old beach house. It was crowded and difficult to do much in the very public light of the motel, no matter how nice it was to have a pool and a nearby fishing pier. Jesse had driven the big semi truck and generator over to the beach and parked it near the house so that Steve could have the Starlighter nearby, "Just to keep an eye on it," he had said with a wink and a smile.

The house had aired out and all the burnt wood had already been removed. In its place were new sights and smells. Unpainted cut planks and new doors took the place of the old ones, with a distinctive wood and paint smell. The girls were happy to be back together instead of having different rooms keeping them apart. They immediately changed into swimsuits and headed to the beach. With all the events that had happened to them, they were at a point where there was little they could do. "Let the adults handle it," proclaimed Aurora, as she strode toward the ocean. "I'm done, no more car chases, no fires, no spies. I'm on vacation." She dove with an arcing swoop into the blue-green water. A school of tiny shining fish leapt out of her way.

Bess couldn't let go nearly as easily. She liked puzzles and challenges, but didn't like not having answers. And she definitely didn't like it when someone tried to hurt her or her friends. But she was on an island where she didn't know her way around. Even if she had her horse, Electra, she had no idea where to go. Like Aurora said, "Let the adults handle it." Bess decided to join Lydia as she walked into the calm Atlantic.

As always, the ocean relaxed her. The salt water lifted her up. Bess floated over the rolling waves. She let the soft sandy ocean bottom wisp across her bare feet. Her long strawberry blonde hair was turning more golden by the moment, before she dove her head under a wave. She came up happily drenched and cooled, with her hair now the color of dark hay. Bess drifted on her back, letting the ocean carry her, just above the water. The ocean filled her ears, taking away all the sounds above.

Bess listened to the new sounds to which she had grown accustomed. The waves washed to the shore, and a soft gravel rush of sound accompanied them as the sand under the waves moved back and forth. Muted cries of delight came from kids in the shore break nearby. A high pitched whine of a propeller screw came from out to sea. Bess closed her eyes, listened, then slowly let the sounds drift away as she ignored everything.

In the back of her mind, she heard another sound. Again she noticed the dull pulsing tone she had heard before. It nagged at her, like it didn't belong. The same sound came to her that she had heard before, the other times she had been in the ocean. Bess never thought to ask about it. She guessed it was just one of those things that happened at the beach. It just seemed so... odd.

Bess stood up out of the water. Just to her north stood the old Sea Breeze Pier. It was unoccupied right at the moment. The strange wave of sharks that washed ashore a few days earlier had done some damage to it. A small crane sat idle on the pier, with tall poles nearby, ready to drive them deep into the sandy shore to anchor the pier back into safety. Bess had water stuck in her ears. She felt the strange sensation of it gurgling and dripping out, as if her hearing suddenly cleared. At that moment, her brain began putting pieces together.

"C'mon," she cried, "Get out! I gotta go talk to Mom. I think I might have discovered something."

Only minutes later Bess was standing in the living room of the old beach house, still dripping salt water onto the rug, as she explained what she had realized to her mother.

"The radio at the haunted house," Bess explained excitedly, "it must have been used to communicate with the ships offshore."

"That seems likely, and obvious," Portia answered. She didn't mean to criticize her daughter. She knew that Bess was building to something and wanted to get to the discovery that was making Bess so excited.

"But they must also be using it to communicate with the shark." Bess looked from person to person.

"Again, a likely hypothesis," her mother added.

"And if they are doing that, we should be able to hear it, if we know where to listen."

Steve jumped into the conversation, "Sure, kiddo, but there are so many frequencies, and we wouldn't know what to listen for. Or when to listen."

"Oh we know where to listen, and I know what to listen for." Now Bess had the confidence in her conviction. Everyone stopped talking to listen.

"First, I've already heard them. They are near our radio frequency. They use regular air-wave noise to mask when they speak. But that's not the bigger part. They have to communicate with the shark. The sounds they use don't go through the air.

"They have to go under the water."

She stopped to let her discovery sink in. Her parents were the first to put the pieces together.

"So we know where to listen," said Steve.

"And the sound would be different than the usual radio signals," added Portia.

"And I've already heard them," finished Bess. The rest looked at her in surprise. "Remember when we were floating around, and we could hear that deep sound in the water? But there were no ships around to make the noise. I think that it's something like that. It's like a radio signal mixed with sonar, a deep sound that is used to either control the shark, or at least send it commands.

"I just heard it now, in the water," she finished.

Steve quickly moved to the radio receiver to turn it on. "See, I remembered that the radio at the haunted house had an antenna that looked a lot like this one. They were listening, and sending, but they could be sending to more than one place. The spies probably took the radio with them when the house burned."

Steve had already turned on the radio and was trying to tune the receiver to see what he could hear. If Bess already heard something, then the broadcast could still be going on. "Wait, go back," Bess commanded. In a narrow bit of frequency, she heard a short thrum of sound. "That! If we heard that underwater, it would probably sound a lot like what I heard in the ocean."

The sound was hard to narrow down. It jumped around in the ether of the radio static, but stayed near the frequency Steve had dialed. "I think it's getting louder," Lydia said offhandedly.

"If it's getting louder," Bess stopped, thinking about what she was about to say.

"Then, it's getting closer."

CHAPTER 20

Waves Of Destruction

For a moment, no one moved or spoke. Then Steve jumped up and grabbed the binoculars off the fireplace mantle and began to run toward the sun deck and the dunes along the seashore. Everyone followed.

In the brightness of the day, the sun glistened off the ocean, as small waves rolled in from far offshore. A small fishing boat, far off to sea, sped to the south, leaving a white trail of churned water in its wake. Steve scanned the ocean with his binoculars, looking for anything. "How are we supposed to see a transparent shark under the water on a sunny day?" he angrily wondered aloud. "Maybe I need to take the Starlighter up."

"Over the water?" his wife huffed. "It was not made to float. I think that would be a risk I'm unwilling for you to take." Steve huffed back, but knew Portia was right. It was dangerous to risk his life and the Starlighter. He would if he had to, but not now, not just to look around. "Look for a wake or a change in the motion of the waves instead," Portia advised her husband.

The kids did their best to scan the ocean, but they had no idea what to look for, either. "Maybe it has moved away," said Aurora. "Should we go listen again?"

"Not yet, let's give it a moment," said Bess. She felt sure that the shark had to be close enough that the signal she heard would be that strong.

"Look!"

It was Portia who made the discovery. Though she would have rather never seen what she saw. Everyone followed her outstretched arm toward the ocean.

Just north of them, out to sea, there was a great change in the color of the water. It was as if a section of the ocean had lifted up ten feet and began to roll in. It gained speed, and rose higher and higher. Bess looked, aghast. She saw the direction the narrow wall of water was going. It was headed right toward the Sea Breeze Pier.

"Oh no," she almost whispered. "The pier..."

"Are there people on there?" Aurora almost whimpered her question. Anyone on the pier would surely be thrown into the ocean.

Jesse had already begun to jump the rail of the sun deck. The pier was too far away, but he felt like he had to try to warn anyone fishing there.

"Wait! Jesse!" Steve cried. He waved at the boy, but Aurora was the one who jumped into action. She took off after him, catching Jesse in a few steps. "NO! It's too dangerous! That wave is too big!"

Steve scanned the pier. "There's no one there. It looks like they are closed to repair it." Jesse relaxed for a moment, then realized he still needed to move people off the beach. The wave kept coming, as if directed straight toward the pier. "Get off the beach!" he yelled at the vacationers. "There's a giant wave, get away from the pier!"

At that moment, the wave struck the end of the fishing pier. The water piled up and sent a huge splash of white spray into the air, overtopping the end immediately. The wave wasn't done. While the front of the wave rolled down the pier, the rest of it, a huge bulk of water, continued to pound into the decking and pilings. The end snapped and fell into the ocean.

Then the rest of the pier gave way. One by one the tall wooden pilings snapped, bent, or were pulled up by the deep but narrow wave. Bess watched as if the pier was being picked apart in slow motion. The wood walkway split down the middle, like a deck of cards unshuffling itself. The pilings were pushed aside to shoot up and out. The waves lifted the black poles out of the water. Even from this distance, Bess could make out the white barnacles that encased the bottom half of the pilings.

The wave finally made its way to the shore. In one motion, as if the raging hand of an angered King Neptune himself swatted out, the wave took out the pilings under the pier house. It collapsed under its own weight and fell to the beach, where the flooding waves picked it back up to slam into the dunes. It took only a heartbeat to turn the building into splinters.

The wave hit the beach like a fire nozzle. Water shot out to the sides and rushed up and down the shore. People were running down the beach in terror. The wooden fragments raced down the sand, carried by a seemingly unending flow of ocean. Most of the vacationers climbed the dunes to escape the flood, while some others tried to outrace the oncoming tide.

Jesse and Aurora were already on the beach, waving at people to get to high ground. The big wave had been incredibly powerful, but narrow. The water kept coming up and up from the powerful offshore surge.

Bess was stunned. She had never imagined there could be destruction of such magnitude, with such a callous disregard for the families on the beach. Parents held their kids in their arms, while they stood on the grassy hills and dunes that barely kept them from the raging tidal wave. While her friends ran down to the beach to see if anyone was injured, she just stood, looking. Then she forced her feet to move as the water finally began to recede.

She looked for people who may be in the water or trapped under sand or the wood from the pier. For a moment, she took in the horror of all the destruction. Bess looked out at where the Sea Breeze pier had been.

It was gone. All gone. Not a single piling stood in the water. The entire pier had been wiped away by the malevolence of the hyaline shark.

CHAPTER 21

The Discovery!

Bess sat on a towel near the dune line as the sun finally started to dip toward the dunes of Jockey's Ridge to the west. The daylight would still be long throughout the summer, but the high sun and wet sand made the day even more uncomfortable than it already had been.

Bess and her friends had spent the better part of the afternoon making sure that people got the care they needed. There were a lot of injured beach-goers across the shore. Some had been caught up in the waves, hit by boards, or cut and scratched by all the flotsam of the destructive wave. Bess felt terrible that the pier had been destroyed. She felt worse that she couldn't tell anyone. She also felt helpless that she could do nothing to stop it.

Bess had seen her friend Vicki come over to look at the destruction. After learning that no one had died, thankfully, the island girl seemed to take the events as a matter of fact. "It's a sad thing, but this happens here. Sometimes we get ships washed up, or a storm knocks out a pier, or a whale beaches. Not usually something this bad, but it's part of livin' here on the island."

Bess took in her comments as one who had lived a life of change. Vacation at the beach should be fun, it had been fun, for her. But living there year round took a different type of commitment. Like living on a ranch in the dry prairie, Bess realized.

Another visitor showed up. Jamie Hodgson, the ichthyologist, wandered onto the shore and found Bess sitting in the sand. "Hi, I heard you saw what happened." She seemed rather bright for walking down a destroyed shore, Bess thought. Bess barely recognized her with a big cap pulled over her head and a long sleeve shirt on.

"Not much to see," Bess said. She knew she couldn't discuss what she knew, and she had little desire to describe what she actually did see. "A big wave came, it hit the pier," she waved her arm at the wide path of destruction still strewn on the beach. A few trucks were trying to pull up the pilings to the empty parking lot. A bulldozer pushed the remains of the pier house into a pile.

"But what caused it?" Jamie wanted to know. "Do you have any idea?" She asked Bess in the tone of a teacher that knew the answer, but wanted the student to say it.

"I have no idea," Bess answered, now wary. "I'm not from here. I don't know much about waves. You probably know more than I do." Bess looked at Jamie, noticing how she held her arm, like it was hurt.

Jamie looked around at the wood scattered across the sand. "Could have been a local displacement, or a little earthquake," she offered. "A bit of the shelf just offshore falls into the deep water, makes a wave, it's called a tsunami. They can be pretty destructive." Jamie reached under her cap and rubbed her forehead. Bess noticed how red and sweaty it was underneath.

Bess only grunted in response to Jamie's theory. She saw her friends wandering up from farther south, so she got up to go see them. "I'm going to go see if they need help. I'm sorry to see you again like this." Bess got up to go as Jamie walked back up over the hill toward the road.

"Weird," Bess said as she watched Jamie go. "That was that fish scientist. She was asking about what happened, but she didn't seem that shaken up by it."

"Maybe she's used to this stuff, storms and waves," Aurora suggested.

"You didn't tell her anything?" asked Jesse.

Bess mimicked zipping her lip and locking it. "Not a peep," she declared. "Yeah, she was really interested in if I knew what had happened. Weird."

They watched her trudge up and over the dune, towards the road and parking lot on the other side. "I got a strange feeling about her," Bess commented. "I feel like I've seen her before."

"Of course you have," said Aurora, "we met her at the marina, and you saw her at the Wright Brothers monument."

"No, it's not that," Bess was tired and hot. Her head wasn't working just right after all the destruction. "I mean, I saw her somewhere else, somewhere..." Bess stopped in mid-sentence and went running up the dune to the sun deck. Her father had left the binoculars sitting on the rail when the pier had fallen. She scooped them up and began looking across the beach, trying to find Jamie.

"There she is," Bess said.

"What are you looking for?" Jesse asked.

"I saw her," Bess insisted, "I know I saw her..." Bess scanned the little parking lot, watching Jamie as she walked. She held her arm to her side with her other hand. Bess thought about what she saw, when Jamie was down on the beach, looking around. Under her hat, she was all red and sweaty, like the cap had left a mark. Or a bruise.

From far away, Bess saw Jamie go up to a car, where a man sat in the driver's seat. The car was old, plain, and white.

It had a pronounced dent on the hood and a big crack in the windshield.

"She's the one from the haunted house!" Bess cried. "She's the person who tried to run Aurora down. She stole my camera from the Starlighter!" More came clear to Bess. "I bet she thought that was the camera we were using. Dad took the big camera out and hid it, but that one was just sitting there.

"She's the Russian spy!"

CHAPTER 22

Spies On The Run

Through the binoculars Bess could see the car start and drive away. Now at least she knew what she could do. She needed to stop them, and stop the attacks from the hyaline shark. Bess eyed the Starlighter, sitting quiet and still next to them on a sandy pad. She could fly them down, but then what? They were dangerous, Bess knew, and willing to hurt or kill anyone. No, she needed help.

Bess ran into the house. "Where are the G-Men?" she almost yelled at her parents, she was so excited. "It's Jamie, that scientist, she's the spy. She's the one who tried to run down Aurora. I recognized her from that night." She let the words fly out of her lips, there was so much she knew and she had to get it all out, to convince her parents.

Portia stopped her quickly. "Hold on, honey. Steve, call them now. Bess, which way did they go?" Bess's mother didn't even start to question her daughter on how she knew all this information. She believed her daughter. Portia always knew to trust Bess when she made decisions, and there was no reason for Bess to make anything up.

"They got in the same white car that was at the haunted house, and at the monument. They went," she had to stop to think, then pointed "that way, south."

"They are coming now," Steve said as he hung up the phone. Bess looked anxiously at her parents, then at Jesse. She was thinking that she should ask him to drive her after the two spies.

"No," said Steve. "We can't let you just go chasing after them on your own." He read Bess's mind. Steve could tell that Jesse would have jumped at the chance to chase down the spies in the old Jeep, but there was no way Steve was going to risk them driving that thing at high speeds. They were made to go off road, but not to race down the highways in a chase. "I'm not going to have you flip that thing over."

Jesse nodded in agreement. "You're right, that Jeep just wouldn't be a good idea.

"The Buick, on the other..."

"No way," Steve answered. "I can't make that decision. Look, this is an island. They can't get but so far. We'll let the pros chase them down, with our help."

It seemed to take forever, but the long black car of agents Marsh and Phillips finally pulled into the drive, where Bess met them. "It's Jamie Hodgson, the ichthyologist, she was the one who tried to run down Aurora at the haunted house! I recognized the car. It's still got the damage from when I dropped that tree on it. I think I hurt her arm and head in the accident."

Agent Marsh thought for a moment, looking at his partner. "If they went south, there's only two directions they can go."

Phillips chimed in. "They could head to Manteo, the airport, or the mainland. That's if they are looking to escape. But they may not know we are on to them."

"Or they went toward Hatteras," added Agent Marsh. "It's a lonely drive, but it's also isolated, with good places to hide. And there's an airstrip down there, as well as lots of places to leave by boat."

"You take Aurora," Bess pushed Agent Phillips toward the Buick, "She knows what the car looks like, and she saw Jamie up close like me. Go toward Manteo.

"We'll go down the road south," she continued with Agent Marsh.

"Good idea," Steve said, "There's a ferry down there past the marina. Even if they are getting on it, that will slow them down. You might catch them in the car line where they cross the inlet."

Agent Phillips took Bess in the Buick, while Agent Marsh drove Aurora and Steve in his big black government sedan. When they reached the end of the beach road, the two cars peeled off into opposite directions.

The big Buick roared down the empty road. Agent Phillips tried to make time up by driving as fast as he could, but the spies had a big head start. As the road stretched out, with no sight of the old white car, Bess's hopes began to sink.

They reached the end of the road, near the open expanse of Oregon Inlet, where the new fishing marina sat. The only way across was by a ferry that took the cars slowly across the choppy water to the islands to the south, including Cape Hatteras and its big black and white candy striped lighthouse. Tourists waited contentedly in the sun, with their cars off, for the ferry to load and unload vehicles.

Bess looked at the many cars waiting in line, while Agent Phillips asked the ferry tenders if they had seen anything like the white sedan. There were plenty of cars, but none like the one the spies had driven.

Agent Phillips found Bess. "These cars have been waiting here for at least 20 minutes, and the crew doesn't remember any white sedan with a broken windshield. Looks like we struck out," he said dejectedly.

They decided to drive back toward home, to hopefully catch up with the others in their search. As

Agent Phillips drove back, Bess stared out the window at the new marina with the many fancy fishing yachts. She stared blankly, deflated at not catching the spies who caused so much damage. Somewhere in her mind, a little voice was starting to speak. Then it yelled.

"Stop!" she screamed. "Over there, in the marina!" Agent Phillips reacted instantly, braking hard and turning the big car into the marina's entrance. He sped down to the parking lot, scanning for the white car that Bess must have seen. He spotted it instantly. The Buick screeched to a stop directly behind the old sedan. Agent Phillips had jumped out almost before the car had stopped. He ran toward the old car, pistol drawn. Bess began to get out, but Agent Phillips waved her back.

It took only seconds, but Agent Phillips discovered that the car was empty. "It looks like they abandoned it," he said as he opened the unlocked door. There was nothing noticeable inside.

Bess looked around, trying to see if she could spot Jamie, or the man she was with. The marina was mostly empty, with a few people walking around or waiting for boats to come back. A few of the big yachts were coming back from fishing trips. They were far off in the inlet, churning through the waves with their catches on ice.

Then Bess spotted something different. Something off.

"Look," she pointed. Agent Phillips followed her gaze. All of the boats were coming in, except one. A boat with a short waterline, slightly different than the bigger flared fishing boats, was racing its way out of the marina. It was heading toward the inlet, and the open water of the Atlantic beyond.

Atop the boat was a distinctive web of metal. "That's the antenna for the radio," Bess said. "That's them. They're trying to get out to sea."

"I bet they are trying to meet up with the Russian fishing fleet," Agent Phillips said. "We need to find a way to stop them." He looked around, but the few boats that were still there were unoccupied; no captains available to make the chase. "Quick, to the car. We might be able to intercept them on the ferry."

Agent Phillips stomped the gas and tore off for the nearby ferry terminal. He was fortunate that the ferry had just unloaded cars and was only beginning to board the waiting travelers heading to Cape Hatteras. Bess watched as he flashed a badge and ID. The ferry crew immediately snapped to attention. They waved off the still boarding cars and let Agent Phillips drive the Buick on board.

With a rumble, the big diesels began to turn the propellers with a determination. Agent Phillips stood at the bow, near the big mesh net meant to keep cars from rolling off the deck in high waves. Bess stood near him. Both were restless with anxiety. They silently willed the big old ferry to go faster.

But the boat with the spies was made for ocean going speed. The ferry was made to go slow and efficiently across the narrow inlet. The ferry captain kept making adjustments to try to intercept the faster boat, but it looked like the spies would pass just in front of them. And then they would be lost to the open Atlantic, with no way to chase them down.

The ferry sounded its horn, trying to flag down the boat. Bess saw that they were getting closer and closer. She hoped that the spies would stop. Maybe they would still have to pretend. She was close enough now that she could make Jamie out at the wheel of the boat.

At that moment, Jamie looked over at the ferry that was desperately trying to signal the spies to stop. She looked at the captain's window, then at the few tourists still waving like there was nothing wrong. Like it was just one more fishing boat going out into the Gulf Stream. Then Jamie looked at the bow, and saw Bess and Agent Phillips standing there.

The boat sped up significantly.

"She saw us," Bess said.

"We're so close," Agent Phillips lamented. He felt inside his jacket, but he was not willing to pull his pistol and start firing from far off while in front of so many people.

Then Bess realized she had her Zap-Gun. She pulled it, looked at Phillips, who nodded in agreement. "It's worth the try," he said, "Can you reach it?"

"We're just about to cross paths," Bess answered. "I think I can get the engine, or at least that radio antenna."

Bess squared herself up on the softly rolling deck. She only needed to get to the hull to put a hole in it, or short out the engine. The two boats got closer and closer. The little fishing yacht was just about to pass only 100 feet in front of the ferry. Agent Phillips ordered everyone else back, and pointed in the direction he wanted the ferry to go. If they couldn't cut the spies off, he wanted to give Bess as many chances as possible to short out the boat's engine.

The spies passed just in front of the ferry bow, with the smaller boat bouncing in the oncoming waves of the Atlantic Ocean. Bess dialed her Zap-Gun up to maximum, with a long, powerful, and tight beam. Then she fired.

The first blast ripped across the water. The bright blue beam was straight, with a glittering reflection trailing it across the inlet water. It hit the spies' boat amidships. The beam cut into the white hull, burning a line across the gunwale.

Bess released the trigger and took new aim. She squeezed the trigger, aiming at the stern. A smoking hole buried itself into the boat, before bursting into a shower of splinters. A huge gaping hole was cut into the spies' ship.

But the damage was doing little to slow the spies in their escape. Bess leaned into the Zap-Gun. She tried to put her own punch in the beam as it tore across the water. A big wave hit the bow of the ferry, from the wake of the spies' boat. The ferry rose slightly, throwing off Bess's aim. But it had an unintended side effect.

Bess's beam ripped across the empty stern of the boat. She saw wood, fiberglass, and cushion stuffing fly into the air. The beam tore through the back of the boat. The diesel engine was now uncovered, and the bright blue beam from Bess's Zap-Gun found a new home. The diesel fuel wouldn't explode, but the machinery would melt and come apart at the high temperatures of the bright static discharge device.

Bess was rewarded with first a dark smoke, then flying bits of machinery, and finally the entire boat began to slow then stop in the water. It bobbed uncontrollably in the rough inlet water. The stern began to take on water.

The ferry steamed up close to the now crippled boat. Agent Phillips stood at the bow, along with two of the ferry crew, who were now armed with their own sidearms. Bess stood ready with her Zap-Gun. Though not nearly as lethal as the pistols the government employees all carried, it would easily cause the two spies to stop in their tracks.

There was little worry about anything the two Russians would do, though. Their boat was sinking, and the ferry, and capture, was the only option left.

As the crew dragged the two spies aboard, Bess had a small look of satisfaction on her face. Jamie, or whatever her real name was, Bess thought, met Bess's gaze with her own devious smile.

"Do you think you've stopped us?" she quietly laughed. "You'll get nothing from us. And you have stopped nothing." She glanced at the rapidly sinking boat. The antenna continued to slowly circle around, even as the rest of the boat sank into the deep channel.

"And now you can't stop it. Nothing can!"

CHAPTER 23

The Ocean Is Awake

Bess had to get a ride back to her beach house from a local Park Service Ranger. Agent Phillips had neither the ability to arrest and keep the two spies in the back seat of a convertible, nor did he want two dangerous people anywhere near a teenage girl. Bess was still worried by what Jamie had said, "You can't stop it. Nothing can..."

The quiet ride back was only interrupted by the occasional banter from the young ranger, asking where Bess's house was. He had little knowledge of what had just happened, how Bess had captured two international spies, and how a rogue crystalline shark was terrorizing the coast. "Are you sure you'll be alright?" he asked as Bess piled out of his truck. The ranger didn't get an answer, but he barely noticed Bess running toward the house when he got a glimpse of the Starlighter standing on its landing pegs in the sandy lot next door.

Bess met her mother, Lydia, and Jesse at the door. She explained that they had caught the spies, as well as the ominous words from Jamie as she had been pulled from the sinking boat. "I don't know if it means they lost control, or we can't stop what it is going to do next," Bess lamented her lack of information. "I'd like to know where the shark is, and if we could stop it."

Jesse and Lydia both looked out the back window, toward the beach and ocean beyond it, thinking about how the shark could be anywhere out there, ready to do more damage. Portia sat back down at the radio, as she began to try to tune back in to the hyaline shark's frequency.

Bess stared out the front window.

"I've got to go looking for it," she declared. "If it's still out there, it's a threat to the beach and the people here. I'm going to fly the Starlighter up and look for it."

"Do you think that's a good idea?" Lydia asked. "I don't know how well that thing would float. Do you really want to fly it over water?"

"I won't, not unless I really have to," Bess insisted. "I'll just take it up over the coast, so I can see farther out. If I can see the shark's wake, or any other boats, I can call Mom and let her know where it is. We can't wait for the G-Men to get back. Every moment we wait is time for the shark to disappear or do more damage."

Bess's mother sat quietly at the radio. She made no argument to stop her daughter, "Because she's right," she would say later.

Bess ran to the Starlighter and climbed in as Jesse now expertly unhooked the big charging cables. When he was safely away in the next yard, Bess watched as he gave a thumbs up. Then she punched the engine launch button. "Up and away," she said to herself.

Bess had flown the Starlighter solo many times, but whenever there was serious work, her mother or father had always been with her. Her dad would always say "Up and away!" in his soft Texas twang, like it was no big deal.

But this was. The Starlighter punched into the blue Outer Banks sky with a burst of white sand under its spinning rings. A quick rattle as the beach pebbles rang out under the high energy chamber where the big pulsing heartbeat of energy pushed the craft into the air was all Bess heard before lifting far off the sandy island.

Once in the sky, the world became soft, quiet, with only the comforting *thumpthumpthump* of the Starlighter's engine firing its heartbeat into the shiny propulsion chamber below Bess. There was no one to talk with in the cockpit. She felt herself get nervous for a moment, wanting to just call her mother for a voice in the ether. Then she calmed, feeling comfortable in the sky. Bess had a task to do. She needed to find the hyaline shark, wherever it was, and somehow stop it.

Hovering over the dunes, she pivoted the Starlighter so she could look out over the water. She made a concentrated effort not to look down. Bess had no fear of heights, but she didn't want to see the remains of the destruction the shark and its controllers caused on the old pier. Not far to the south, she could easily see another wooden pier jutting out into the Atlantic, and then to the north, a similar one. Below her, she knew, there was nothing but broken timbers from the hyaline shark's terrifying hydraulic vortex shot from its mouth.

She scanned the open waters. Bess wasn't entirely sure what to look for. Maybe a fin, but the crystal dorsal fin would be difficult to spot. "It might make some kind of wake," she thought to herself. Several boats were out on the water. A few fishing boats were pulling in nets, and two bright white charter yachts were speeding quickly to the south and Oregon Inlet.

"All of them are going south," she noticed. She realized why. Just to the north, and steaming in fast, was a bright orange and white ship. It was large, and its size made it look deceptively slow. But Bess could see the churning waves on its bow. The big ship was steaming hard in toward the coast. Bess recognized it immediately.

"The Russians," she whispered the words, even though no one was there to hear her. The big trawler was the same one that she photographed. It was the one that was launching and retrieving the hyaline shark. And it was closing in on the shore. The Russian trawler was far in from the usual twelve mile international limit.

"They must be trying to get their shark back," she realized. Bess was able to lock the power collective of the Starlighter for a moment, which allowed it to hover very still. The outer ring hummed at high speed, keeping the craft steady. With one hand free, Bess used binoculars to look more closely at the big trawler.

On the deck she could see people running about. One side held two large cranes, and a net, just like in the photo she had taken. On the bow was a small dish and a rapidly revolving radio antenna. It was slightly bigger than the one at the old haunted house, but identical in every other way. "That's how they control it," Bess figured. "They are trying to call it back."

Without any weapons, as the Starlighter was not meant for shooting at enemy planes or ships, she had little at her disposal. All the Starlighter was, was a very fast flying craft.

Very fast, Bess thought. "Faster than anything out here, faster than a shark."

She put her binoculars down, then took control of the Starlighter.

Bess dipped the controls, letting the leading edge, which was wherever she looked, lean down and forward. The ring of winglets that controlled the flight opened and closed, letting the Starlighter lose altitude, but gain speed. Bess had speed to burn now.

"It's a risk," she thought, "but I have to do it." Bess was now flying out over the water. It was something her father had lightheartedly warned her. "This thing doesn't float," he had said. If anything happened, she didn't know if she would be able to get out. She would be miles away from land. And there would be Russian spies all around her.

And an invisible shark that was sixty feet long somewhere.

Bess twisted the power collective hard.

At one hundred feet, she began to level off. The Starlighter felt heavy as it compressed the air under it as it neared the ocean. Bess sank in her seat. The feeling was comforting to Bess. She knew and expected it as she nestled herself in her cockpit seat. Now she was barely skimming above the water. When she looked over her shoulder, she could see the rapidly disappearing beach and shoreline vanish in a tail of water as the Starlighter sucked up the ocean behind her.

"Bess?! Bess?!" the radio called, "What are you doing?" Her mother was reaching out. She probably saw Bess leave the safety of land and head out, but may not know the Russians were just offshore.

"Don't worry, Mom," Bess depressed the radio button on her controls. "I see the ship that controls the shark. I've got to stop them. Don't worry, they will be the ones who get a little wet. Over and out." Bess signed off with finality. She had no time to tell her mother of her plan.

The Starlighter closed in on the moving trawler at incredibly high speed. At first, she could just see some sailors pointing. When she twisted up the throttle to her highest speed, they began to run. Bess had only seconds to do this, and had to time her approach just right.

She softly tweaked the controls, eyeing her altitude so that she would clear the deck of the ship. Bess worried about those cranes. They could reach up and snatch her out of the sky if she got too close and ran into them. But she didn't want to lose the fast moving wall of water she had behind her.

It was only seconds now. She was moving at five hundred miles an hour, maybe more. The speed made maneuvering difficult, but the Starlighter could do it, she knew. She had done this before.

"Just not over water," she thought.

Right before she reached the orange ship, Bess pulled the controls hard up toward her and twisted the power collective down. It took all the thrust out from under the Starlighter, and lifted her leading edge up toward the sky. It was almost as if she stopped right above the Russian trawler, then stood the craft up on its edge. Before it had completely stopped, Bess spun the collective back to full power, dumping electricity out the big chamber under her. A bright glow of purple and blue pulsed out from under the winglets and all around her.

But the big electrical pounding was not what Bess had planned. It may have shorted out some components, but what came next was what she really wanted.

The wave took a moment, just a few beats of her heart, or a quick breath. Then the huge trailing wall of water, like a wake from a speedboat, crashed directly into the trawler.

Only instead of a speedboat it was the wake of a five hundred mile per hour flying ship.

The wave pounded into the side of the trawler. Immediately the ship lurched to the side. Its engines stopped from the sheer stress. If Bess could have opened a window she would have heard the sound of a hundred alarms all going off at once. The wave had knocked the ship sideways.

But that wasn't enough. The wave kept coming. More water poured over the deck. There just was nowhere else for it to go. As Bess lifted up, she turned the Starlighter to see her work. The big wave kept covering the deck, even as the ship tried to right itself. On the deck, the cranes were flattened. "Try hoisting up that shark now," Bess said out loud, nearly shouting it to the ship and its nefarious crew.

She scanned the bow. That's where she really wanted to cause the damage. Near the front, dripping with water and foam, the radio antenna lay in ruins, twisted metal broken all along the deck. The big dish was nowhere to be seen at first. Then Bess saw it floating on the port side of the ship, before it slipped into the green churned water and disappeared.

Bess lifted high up over the stricken ship. She looked at the helm, the tall tower toward the back, and the stack just behind it. The engine seemed to struggle. Bess saw first a stream of white smoke and steam pour from the stack, then a dark phlegmy cough of thick soot shot out. The cloud hovered over the bridge like a cursed fog. It was s fitting moment for the disgraced spies and their ship.

Bess had to get out of there and back toward land. She leaned the Starlighter toward the beach, and away from the trawler. In a moment of clarity, she called on the radio to her mother.

"Mom? Mom? I'm heading in. Over." She hoped her mother was still there. Portia could have been out watching everything from the sundeck. At least everyone would know she was safe and heading inland.

A familiar voice came on the radio, but it wasn't her mother. "Hey kiddo, you alright?" Bess's father had returned to the house.

"Oh yeah, never better, Dad!" Bess fairly sang over the radio. "I took out the controls for that shark. They were running it from that trawler."

"We know, kiddo." her father didn't sound happy. He didn't seem mad, either. Bess thought he would be thrilled she knocked out the spy ship and their terrible weapon. "Bess, look around," he asked.

"The shark is still out there," Steve continued. "The kids say it's somewhere to the south of us. Over."

Bess let the Starlighter go into a hover. She looked to the south. There were no other ships out. They had all been scared away by the big Russian trawler.

Bess spotted the shark easily. It still was below the water, but only barely. It was going in slow circles, mindless as it swam at high speed with no master to control it. It was easy to spot because it made a slow circular wake as it made its way closer and closer to the beach. Worse than that, it continually pulsed out a huge vortex of water from its gaping jaws. Bess looked at the shark, then the direction it was headed.

"Dad!" she cried out as she called on the radio. "You have to get the gang down to the beach! It's headed toward the other pier!"

CHAPTER 24

Crushing Jaws

Bess could see the shark still out to sea, slowly spiraling toward the long wooden structure of Jennette's Pier. Already, small churning waves were building up in the deep, heading toward shore. She twitched the controls to head toward it, still unsure of how to stop it.

If she even could.

On the pier, she could see the people fishing. Lines stretched from tiny poles out into the ocean. They had no idea of the size of the fish approaching them. Bess had no way to warn them, either. She had to find some way to send the terrifying robotic shark back out to sea. Even that didn't guarantee it wouldn't come back.

The Starlighter flew back out to sea to chase down the hyaline shark. "Maybe I can do the same thing to it that I did to the ship," Bess thought. It took only a minute to fly out to where the shark approached the shore, but to Bess the time seemed to be terrifyingly long. She only had a finite amount of time, and power, to do something.

The shark continued to circle, getting closer and closer. Bess tried to time a low pass just in front of the shark's path, but she missed on her first try. The transparent beast simply dove under any wave she made. It was a simple but unstoppable defense set into the machine shark's controls.

She watched as the shark came around in a circle to get closer to the beach. It would only be minutes before it reached the pier with its devastating vortex wave. On its second pass, Bess simply parked the Starlighter over where the shark would cross. She opened the winglets to let the Starlighter lazily spin, while pouring electrical power out of the propulsion chamber. The ocean just beneath her turned into a boiling foamy pot of salt water. The hyaline shark plowed mindlessly into the maelstrom and disappeared.

Bess pulled up on the collective to make the Starlighter rise. "Maybe that has done it," she said as she quickly wiped sweat from her hand. The cockpit had become thick with still air, all hot and humid. She could smell the ozone from the buildup of electricity under her in the wide shining combustion chamber. The Starlighter still *thumpthump*'ed with its heartbeat, but at a slightly slower pace than Bess's. She was glad for that. Bess looked at the energy output and the small black dial with a white needle jiggling on it. Even though she had only been flying for less than ten minutes, all the high speed maneuvers had used up a large amount of the Starlighter's batteries.

Just then the hyaline shark breached high out of the water behind her. "All I did was push it closer to the pier," Bess sighed, dejected.

"I need to get the people off the pier!" Bess said. "But how?" She was afraid if she parked the Starlighter in the sky, more people would go out on the pier just to look. She lifted up and spun the Starlighter to see the pier now just west of her. She had lost track of the shark, which was completing yet another terrifying circle toward the beach. "They have to at least see the shark coming," Bess thought.

Then she saw the movement from the pier. "Yes!" she screamed, loud and echoing in the Starlighter. People were running off the pier. They dropped their poles and headed in. She could even see a few people waving at the others, directing them to get off. "At least the people will be safe," she thought.

Looking toward the pier, Bess didn't notice the hyaline shark making its next pass until it neared her. It wouldn't hit the pier, but it would come close. "Those waves it makes are really going to churn the pier up," she thought, helpless to do anything but watch. The shark had released one of its horrid water vortexes, which narrowly missed the pier. It wasn't building up power with one blast. Like it was on autopilot, or a timer, it made the waves at regular intervals. They were smaller, but still powerful and dangerous.

Bess hoped everyone got off the pier. She looked back and saw that everyone was off the end. Or almost everyone. Two figures stood at the very end of the pier. It was a wide, open spot, making the pier look like it was shaped like a T with a very narrow top. The shark began to pass just outside of the end of the pier. Then the two people still on the end reached out.

Bess saw two bright blue bolts of light hit the shark and the water as it passed by. "Lydia and Aurora!" Bess recognized them now. Her two friends had run to the end of the pier with their Zap-Guns to help stop the shark. About thirty feet from them stood a tall blond. "That has to be Jesse," Bess realized. They had seen where Bess had gone, or heard her call on the radio with her father, and gone to save the people on the pier.

"And now they are putting themselves in danger to stop the shark." Bess worried about her friends, but she knew she would have been doing the same thing.

Blue light beams poured out over the water until the shark swam out to sea. It had come so close to the pier the last time. "They have to stop it now," Bess thought.

For a moment, Bess was distracted by a small orange light on her control panel. It was a warning light, saying she was starting to run low on power. It usually meant about ten minutes of flying time, but Bess had been draining the Starlighter of its electric charge. "No time to worry about that now," she said in her head. "When the red light comes on, it's time to coast in, but I'm not going anywhere before that." She had to keep track of the shark. She had to help warn her friends.

This time the shark was heading toward the pier. As it turned, there was no doubt it would either hit the pilings, or somehow magically pass through. Bess hoped it would miss the pier, or maybe just break apart in the impact. She watched, helpless. As it turned toward the pier, again, blue bolts of lightning poured out at it. The water steamed, and Bess could see bits of the strange crystal structure start to peel off or crack.

Then the shark let loose one of its wave vortexes, right into the pilings of the pier.

The waves ripped through the pier, just before the very end where Lydia, Aurora, and Jesse stood. The big telephone pole sized braces all tore off and fell into a churned jumble. They were half attached and half broken into giant splinters. The shark headed toward the pier with its broken and open path underneath the walking deck. Just as it looked like the shark would pass through, it got caught in the tangle of sticky black wood. The pilings acted like a gruesome spider web, with their barnacle covered pieces ripping into the hyaline shark. Bits of glass were scratched and shredded off as the shark tried to power through. The mindless machine didn't think. It just kept trying to put power to the water jets at the back of it.

The shark attempted a leap. It was angled up by a wave, and slightly free, as a burst from the powerful engines tried to lift it out of the water. The animated struggling shook the pier's remains. With an agonizing silent slowness, the pier deck fell down on top of the shark. Bess could see only the shark's giant open mouth peering out from beneath the wooden pier. In causing the destruction of Jennette's Pier, the hyaline shark had trapped itself.

Then Bess realized that her friends were now cut off. They were trapped at the end of the pier, and the shark was slowly, thoughtlessly, shaking the pier to bits.

There was no way anyone else would get there in time. Bess punched the throttle to get over the pier. She was the one who had to save them. They had stopped the shark. She wasn't going to let them fall into the water with that thing as it thrashed the pier to death.

"I can't land there easily," Bess knew. The tiny end of the pier was barely big enough to hold the Starlighter, and it was shaking with every movement of the hyaline shark beneath it. If she came down under power, the big electrical pulses would shake the pier to bits, and send her friends flying into the water. She had to land it unpowered.

Bess had done this before, fortunately. Actually, the Starlighter was designed to do just that. With a pull of an emergency lever, the winglets opened at an angle, and the Starlighter would slowly spiral its way down to a soft landing.

But it would take time. The Starlighter would land like a feather, but float just as slowly, too.

It didn't help when the little amber light turned red and started beeping. Bess was running out of power.

She twisted down the power. Now over the end of the broken pier, Bess reached for the emergency lever and pulled it. All power stopped. The heartbeat went silent. With a clank, all the winglets opened around the circular cockpit. Bess simply kept one hand on the controls to give tiny adjustments to the Starlighter as it floated gently to the pier.

Bess had no such gentle feelings. No matter how lightly she touched down, the Starlighter still weighed a lot. She had no power and no ability to lift off if anything went wrong. "Not that I would leave my friends," she thought. "No way I'm abandoning them."

Bess could see Lydia, Aurora, and Jesse all in one corner of the pier as she began to land. They disappeared from sight as the outer ring still spun silently to keep the Starlighter balanced. She knew the outer edge would be higher than the pier railing. It would be terrible to saw into the wood at the last instant. "Or into my friends," she thought gravely.

Bess tried to keep the Starlighter level as it touched down evenly. She immediately got up to open the hatch to let her friends in. The pier shook with yet another lurch from the shark. It felt like the whole end leaned to one side. She saw Lydia stumble and slide before Aurora grabbed her roughly by the arm to pull her in.

Jesse was the last to get in. With the sound of the slamming hatch, he yelled, "Go! Go!"

Bess was terrified that the Starlighter wouldn't launch. She had no idea how much power was left, and she needed a lot to get the ship up. She felt another shudder as the pier moved beneath her. More of the pilings gave way, and suddenly the end of the pier lurched to her left. It was collapsing under the weight of the Starlighter!

Bess punched the power button and the launch button at the same time, while twisting madly at the collective to pour all the energy into the electric combustion chamber beneath her and her friends.

She felt a wonderful second of relief, as the Starlighter punched its way into the air. The feeling was familiar, comforting.

Then the entire pier end fell out from beneath her.

The blast of electricity had pushed just as hard on the wooden pier as it had on the Starlighter. The ship lifted up only ten feet before the pier fell out from below. Suddenly, with nothing below them, there was nothing for the superheated air to use to support the Starlighter. The ship, its pilot, and passengers, all began to fall.

Bess did the only thing she could do. React. She leaned the Starlighter forward. Angling away from the falling pier, she headed toward the open ocean. The Starlighter still fell, but now it had some impetus. It was falling forward, not down.

Lydia clung to one of the chairs as she looked out the window. She could only utter a wordless "Uuuuhhnnngggg..." as the leading edge of the Starlighter's ring got closer and closer to the water. If it hit, the spinning ring would cut through the water, throwing the balance off the Starlighter. "And we'll all be in the drink," Bess thought.

She pulled up on the control, silently willing the Starlighter to rise. She watched as the edge got close, then closer, then softly cut through a low rolling wave.

Then the ship lifted.

Bess got it up into the air, and began a soft easy arc toward the beach. She had been so worried about just getting the Starlighter off the pier, she had not heard anything but what her own mind was telling her. She hadn't even heard that ringing in her ears.

The one that was telling her she was out of energy.

One thousand feet away and forty feet up, the Starlighter went silent again. "This time for good," Bess said to herself.

There was nothing left to do but hope they would make it to the beach. Bess yanked the emergency handle once more. The Starlighter's winglets clanked open softly. From just outside, a soft whisper of an ocean breeze whistled around the silent cockpit.

"Well," Bess said, a lopsided smile on her face, "You all wanted to hit the beach!"

CHAPTER 25

Holding Down The Sand

"Strap in," Bess yelled at her friends. She had not been able to speak to them until this moment. With the Starlighter silent and slowly spinning toward shore, her urgent shout felt out of place. Bess knew it would still be close to get the Starlighter to land.

"We're going to make it to the sand, right?" Lydia found her voice with a shaking question. "I mean, this thing... it can't float, right? It's all metal. We need to make it to the beach!"

"Sit down, Lydia," bellowed Aurora. She roughly grabbed her friend and flung Lydia toward an empty cockpit chair. The Starlighter spun lazily, but the angle it was at made moving difficult. Aurora jumped to the other chair and struggled with the thick mesh belts.

Jesse had no chair to sit in. The Starlighter had only three pilot seats. But his work on the ground crew mean he knew a secret. He grabbed at a small tray folded into the middle console. It snapped down with a click, and Jess grabbed the small lap belt and pulled it tight. The little jump seat wasn't meant for hard landings, but it would keep him from being flung across the cockpit.

"Let Bess fly," Aurora continued a little more coolly. She felt bad about yelling at her friend, but the danger and panic had stirred them all up.

Lydia didn't care. She just wanted to make sure they didn't sink in the ocean.

"We'll make it to the shallows, at least," Bess said. She didn't want to crash into the water, and she still wasn't sure if they would make it, but she wasn't going to tell her friends that. "We'll be okay. Jesse, be ready to get everyone out."

"I'm on it," he said, one hand held on his belt to unbuckle, the other tight on a nearby handle.

Bess felt the winds and waves under her. She tried to angle the Starlighter a little toward the land. "Anything to get a few more feet," she urged the ship on in her mind. "C'mon, c'mon..."

A wave crashed under her. The salt air and a slash of water sloshed on the underside of the Starlighter. Bess was so close.

With her last bit of hope, she tried pressing the electric launch button again. A small pop, then nothing. If it lifted the ship, it was feet.

Or inches.

Bess finally saw the beach below her. On each side of her, people stared in wonder at the incoming strange sight of the Starlighter. "Just a few more feet," she begged.

With her last bit of altitude left, Bess pitched her controls forward. It was a desperate act to keep the Starlighter out of the crashing waves. She hoped to skid it in, but the leading edge was too far down. The down angle had given her speed, but sacrificed the last bit of altitude. With a lurch and a soft crunch, the Starlighter nosed its edge into the seagrass covered dune. It was wedged in at an angle. The ship propped up, just above the sand.

Inside, everyone leaned into their safety belts. Jesse was the first to unbuckle, just as he promised. He immediately tumbled out of his seat, away from the hatch, and slammed into the back of Bess's chair.

"Ooof!" he let out a soft complaint and a soft cry.

"Are you alright?" Bess tried to turn but was still stuck in the chair.

"Yup," Jesse said. He pulled himself up and put a foot on the back of Bess's chair, then jumped for a handle and the hatch.

It took some work, but the three girls and one boy crawled their way out of the Starlighter, and then jumped to the soft sand of the Nags Head beach. Lydia rolled in it, on her knees, happy to be on land, dry or otherwise.

Bess walked out from under the Starlighter. It seemed not overly damaged, but the big metal disc stood ominously over her, and she wasn't going to be there if it started to fall. She looked over at the remains of Jennette's Pier. The end was a jagged mess. Timbers, planks, and pilings all stuck out at odd angles in the deep water. At the very end, the broken decking sat like a splintered roof. Bess could make out the remains of the hyaline shark. It was broken in the middle. Its mouth open but empty, lifeless. The terrifying machine was now and forever no longer a threat. Bess and her friends had risked their lives to stop it. She had crashed the Starlighter in the process, and probably caused a lot of other problems too, but then Bess thought, "It was still worth it. That thing can't do any more damage."

Bess looked back at her friends. They all stood admiring their own part in stopping the hyaline shark and the spy ring that had attacked the Outer Banks. Jesse was bruised, Lydia covered in sand and still shaken, Aurora still looked a little mad, but they all had the same attitude of defiance on their faces.

"No one messes with the Zap-Gun Rangers," Aurora said, hands on her hips.

Bess turned around to see people coming toward her. In the front of the group was her father and mother. For a second, Bess frowned, then tried to smile sheepishly at her dad. Steve came up close and stopped in front of her.

Then he put his hand on her shoulder and said, "Any landing you can walk away from, huh, kiddo?"

Three days later, Bess and Lydia stood knee deep in the low breaking waves of the Atlantic shore. Lydia had found a child's toy ball, deflated and flattened, washed up on the beach. She had picked it up intending to throw it away, when she crushed it between her hands. Without thought, she had tossed it across the water and the thing had skipped through the tiny waves. Now she and Bess had fun flinging the crushed plastic ball to each other in the shallows.

"I'm glad those G-Men were able to get us another week here," Lydia yelled.

Agents Marsh and Phillips had used considerable pull of their mysterious agency to do a lot in the days after Bess and her friends had stopped the hyaline shark. The Russians had been unhappy politically when their ship was "attacked," as they had claimed. Until it was pointed out that they were in US waters and conducting acts of sabotage. They had gotten quiet very fast after that. "No more Russian fishing boats offshore," Bess had pointed out.

A crane had to come and lift the Starlighter out of the sand. It was fortunately undamaged, but needed some care. The simplest solution turned out to be the best. It was carried across the island to a barge and shipped up the sound to a rather secret military base that had the tools to do some of the repairs needed. Portia benefited from both the respect of a lot of engineers as well as still having Top Secret clearance from her days working at Los Alamos long ago. When Bess asked where the Starlighter went, her father winked and said cryptically, "The Flying Saucer Repair Shop." He was the only one who could get away with calling the Starlighter a "Flying Saucer" around Bess.

There was little left to do. Cleanup of the lost and damaged piers began quickly. No one wanted reminders of what had happened. "Do you think the G-Men will try to cover this up like they did with..." Aurora had looked around before continuing her question, "*you-know who* from *you-know-where*?"

"I doubt it," Bess answered. "Let's face it, everyone saw it, and there really is nothing to hide. We all know it was the Russians, and it isn't like we've ever been trying to hide the Starlighter. We flew it across the country to have it here for Orville Wright's birthday."

So, at least for a few more days, the kids had comfortable and relatively stress free vacation time coming to them. Bess enjoyed being able to ride horses with Vicki again. She had ridden down to Bodie Island Lighthouse, where they had a picnic at the black and white striped light, before heading home into a beautiful orange twilight.

Now, it was time for a relaxing day at the beach. Bess played catch with Lydia. Jesse sat in a chair on the beach. He wanted to join in, but found that relaxing in the big folding cloth chair was easier, as he favored the big purple bruise on his side. Jesse pressed a cold glass bottle of Coca-Cola against it.

"Does it still hurt bad?" Steve asked the young man.

"Not much," Jesse said, hiding a grimace. "I'm glad I didn't break anything. I'll be fine by the time we have to do the trip back."

"Oh, no!" Steve insisted. "You and the girls have done enough. You are going back with Bess's mom, first class. I'll get one of my pals to fly in the Starlighter with me."

"I concur," said Portia. She sat next to Steve, calm and smiling behind her bright white sunglasses and bright red lipstick. Her hair was neat as ever, in a jet black ponytail that was more in tune with vacation than her usual shiny bun. She took a sip from her own soda and said, "Now, stop talking and start having more fun. Maybe find an Elvis Presley song on that new radio of yours."

Jesse tried to put a half smile, half snarl on his face as he said, "Uh-that's alright, mama," but his poor attempt only made Portia laugh and spit out her drink.

"Yeah, okay, maybe I'm not Elvis. But Elvis never fought a shark."

Bess and Lydia came running up to their towels. They shook their hair, sending ragged drops of seawater all over Jesse and the parents. Bess didn't get the response she thought she would. Her mother said, "Oh, that feels good. It's so hot. I think I am going to have to go for a swim."

Aurora was just cresting the sand dune with a basket and cooler in her hands. She had gone to a nearby grocery store to get some more snacks and drinks. Bess walked up the hot sand to help carry everything down.

"Hey, I got us some more soda pop!" Aurora announced. "I'm going to plop down on my towel, drink a cold soda real fast, and not do anything, *any thing*, for the rest of vacation! I'm going to sleep out here. You're gonna have to drag me onto the plane home!"

Bess laughed and smiled at Aurora's happy commitment to doing nothing. That was what the vacation was supposed to truly be about. Bess thought back to when she first arrived, and how the boy that drove them to the beach had told her that the house was haunted.

"Wow," she thought quietly, "To think that not long ago all I had to worry about was if I would see a ghost somewhere."

Aurora and Bess walked up to the chairs and towels strewn across the sand. Bess walked ahead, hurrying to get to the cooler sand near the shore.

Aurora slowed as she got closer.

Bess said, "Who needs another Coke?"

A hand came up from one of the chairs as Steve Truly asked for a soda. "I'll take one," he said.

Aurora stopped and stared at the backs of the chairs. "How are you here?" she said, softly.

Aurora walked around the two beach chairs where Steve and Portia sat. "How did you get here?"

"Are you alright, dear?" asked Portia as she looked over her sunglasses. "Has the heat gotten to you?"

Aurora stood still, her mouth slightly open. Then she squinted and shook her head. "Seriously, I just saw you two when I came by the house. I saw your shadows in the kitchen.

"At least I think it was you."

Steve looked at Bess, and Bess looked back at her father. The two said nothing as they read each other's minds.

"Ummmm..." Steve started to speak, "maybe... we might want to go back to that hotel for the rest of the week."

About The Author

Joe Sledge is the author of the Bess Truly series of young reader adventure books. His nonfiction collection includes the *Did You See That?* series of weird travel guides. He has also authored a collection of ghost tale books on North Carolina and the Outer Banks coast.

Joe is a North Carolina native, having grown up on the Outer Banks, as well as attending the University of North Carolina-Chapel Hill. After traveling extensively across the country as well as internationally, he moved back to NC with his wife. Joe currently runs Gravity Well Books, his publishing company. When not writing he spends as much time as possible with his wife and daughter exploring and being outside.

9 789898 801713 4